LUPO

AND THE LOST PIRATE OF KENSINGTON PALACE

THE ADVENTURES of a ROYAL DOG

LUPO

AND THE LOST PIRATE OF KENSINGTON PALACE

ABY KING

Illustrated by Sam Usher

Hodder
Children's
Books

First published in Great Britain in 2016
by Hodder Children's Books

1

A Catalogue record for this book is available from the British Library

ISBN: 978 1 444 92157 1

Typeset in Egyptian 505 BT Light by Avon DataSet Ltd,
Bidford-on-Avon, Warwickshire

Printed and bound by Clays Ltd, St Ives plc

MIX
Paper from
responsible sources
FSC® C104740

The paper and board used in this book are made from wood from responsible sources.

Hodder Children's Books
A division of Hachette Children's Group
Carmelite House
50 Victoria Embankment
London EC4Y 0DZ

www.hachette.co.uk
www.theadventuresoflupo.com

For my brother Oliver, thanks for all the adventures
we shared as children.
And for
Prince George, Princess Charlotte and, most
importantly,
Lupo, thank you for inspiring me.

Whisper
Whisper not too loudly
May your dreams be always filled with the chase
Roam free dear friend – for miles and miles
May your heart forever guide you home
To us,
Your family

Contents

1
A Discovery

Kensington Palace was abuzz with activity. Lupo walked around the palace watching the butlers, maids, housekeepers, footmen and cooks all busy at work. It was rare that he was allowed out of Apartment 1A, but today someone had left the front door slightly open and Lupo couldn't resist exploring. He watched the staff rushing around, making sure that everything had been perfectly arranged just the way the royal family liked it. Nobody noticed him as he trotted by, his long black tail wagging merrily.

He came to the main staircase and sat down to look at the painted walls. He had always been in such a hurry that he had never stopped to admire the staircase that displayed the finest art. The hand-painted people leant over balconies and watched the

1

busy palace below. In the light from the lanterns that floated next to the stairs the people looked almost alive as they talked, pointed and laughed.

Lupo was about halfway up the staircase when someone, or rather something, caught his eye. At first it looked like a shadow behind one of the painted people, then it moved. Lupo stood up and peered forward, his ears lifting so that he could hear better.

'Who's there?' he asked. But no one answered.

He could see a strange figure hiding behind the people in the pictures – and he could just make out a large black hat – when all of a sudden it moved again. Now he could see more clearly. It was a ghost. Lupo was sure he knew about all the ghosts in the palace. Kitty, the palace cat, had told him about them all, but she had never mentioned a ghost like this one.

He walked slowly up the stairs and came to a stop on a black-and-white tiled landing. He was now the furthest he'd ever been able to venture outside of the apartment he shared with his family.

'Hello, are you there?' he barked softly, not wanting to scare away the mysterious ghost. 'You can come out, I'm not afraid of you.'

Prince George was on his little red and blue bike

at the bottom of the staircase. He too had found his way out of the apartment. The little boy smiled and waved up to his pet dog.

Lupo ran down the stairs, leaving the ghost behind. He whistled and chomped, using the special language he shared with the prince to say, 'Let's explore the basement.'

Unbeknownst to them both, Lupo and George were being followed by the sad palace ghost in the black hat. It floated behind them as George raced down empty corridors. The little prince was very speedy on his bike. Lupo had to run fast to keep up with the royal boy.

On their way to the basement, they bumped into the housekeepers who were too busy checking one side of a large blanket to notice at least twenty baby palace mice running around on the other side of the blanket chasing each other!

'Make sure it's properly folded,' bossed the large housekeeper, 'and that the napkins and tablecloths have been ironed just the way the Duchess likes them. Her Majesty is coming for tea and I want everything to be just right!' George whizzed under the blanket, causing the housekeeper to jump. 'Hey, is that Master George?' Lupo raced after him. 'And what is that dog doing out?' shouted the housekeeper. 'Quick, catch them!'

Kitty the palace cat was curled up in the corner of the kitchens. She was on Cook's rocking chair. Her tiny black nose twitched, enjoying the scent of freshly baked bread, sticky sweet desserts and roast chicken. She was moments from slipping off into a pleasant sleep when she was awoken by the little prince and Lupo racing into the kitchen. Lupo barked excitedly.

'What's all this noise? And will someone please explain to me why Prince George is riding his bike through my kitchen?' cried the Head Chef, shaking her fists. 'Get that dog out of here!'

Kitty stretched and yawned silently before leaping off the chair. With nothing better to do she decided to follow the pack of palace staff who were now desperately trying to catch the royal toddler and his dog.

'Lupo is in big trouble. If Cook catches him he's had it,' she muttered to herself. 'I'd better see if I can help them escape her clutches.'

Kitty had been a stray when she'd arrived at

Kensington Palace. She'd been adopted by the staff so she was accustomed to every inch of the famous London residence. This meant that she had her own ways of getting around that no one but she knew. With things heating up in the kitchen there was only one way out for Lupo and George, and she knew exactly how to help them. Which was why she crawled on her belly under the roaring palace stoves and into the space between the kitchen walls. She ran all the way to the food elevator on the far side of the room, flinging the back of it open and waited for the opportunity to grab Lupo and George as they ran past.

Lupo saw Kitty waving from inside the small lift. 'George, the lift. That's how we can escape!'

George giggled because this was exactly the kind of mischief-making he liked most. Nanny had joined the pack of palace staff. George heard her voice and jumped off his bike, diving into the lift with Lupo right behind him.

'ARGH! NANNY'S COMING!' shouted George.

'Relax. I've got this covered. Hold on!' Kitty replied smugly.

Nanny and Cook had made it to the front of the

pack and were almost at the lift when Kitty pushed a big red square button on the side of the lift. WHOOSH! it went, flying upwards. George cheered with joy while Lupo tried to steady himself.

'You forget, I know every inch of this palace and all the very best escape routes!' said Kitty. 'Next stop, the palace staterooms. Level Two.'

Lupo had never been to the staterooms before so when Kitty opened the lift he was shocked to see that the room was full of mice. Hundreds of them ducked in and out of holes in cupboards and floorboards.

Bernie the Head Mousekeeper was giving out her instructions. 'Remember, Mice, we must not be seen! So make sure that you keep your distance! If one of those humans sees us, we have all had it. They don't like our kind so watch out for traps. Now, Angus and Guy, don't think I didn't see you two running up the curtains last night! Trying to "catch tail" is not a game I will accept in my dining room!' Lupo smiled at Angus and Guy, who looked stunned at having been found out. Bernie wasn't finished. 'Right, first duty is to make sure that the pillows are fully stuffed. Clive, don't think I didn't know that you have been up to no good pulling out the stuffing all winter!'

George jumped out of the lift, sending all the mice scattering. Lupo watched as the little prince ran around the room, trying to catch the surprised creatures.

Kitty was the last to jump out and for the first time ever she wasn't remotely interested in the mice. 'Lupo, did you see the ghost – the one in the black hat?'

Lupo looked around the room. 'Where is it?' Kitty didn't answer because she was in stealth mode. Lupo continued, 'I saw it on the staircase earlier! Who is it, Kitty? You never mentioned him before.'

'*Ssssshhhh!*' Kitty interrupted Lupo. She was creeping along the floor looking for the strange ghost. 'It was in the corner of the room. I saw it just as we opened the lift door. Never seen it before, which is odd, because I know all the ghosts in the palace and that one looked pretty old to me. Whoever he is, he doesn't belong in Kensington Palace, that's for sure – better suited to a boat, I think.'

'A boat?' asked Lupo quietly.

'Yes, he was wearing an old captain's hat,' answered Kitty.

'You're right – he looked like a pirate!' shouted Lupo. 'Just like an old pirate!'

'SSSSSSHHHHHHHH,' hushed Kitty. 'He went that way!'

Lupo, Kitty and George looked in every one of the magnificent staterooms. They even looked behind the long silk curtains (and caught Angus and Guy playing instead of working). But there was no sign of the mysterious ghost.

'We've looked everywhere,' said Lupo, 'it's gone.' Half of his body was under a priceless table and Angus and Guy were having lots of fun trying to catch his wagging tail.

Kitty's whiskers twitched. 'Something isn't right,' she said, sitting on the floor, her claws scrunching at the red carpet. 'A strange pirate ghost just suddenly appears in the palace. It doesn't add up.'

Lupo batted Angus and Guy away with one swipe of his long black tail, which reduced them to fits of giggles. 'Kitty, it's just a ghost. It may not mean anything. But you're right . . . it is a little odd.'

They agreed to carry on searching. This meant that they would have to go further into areas of the palace where animals were not allowed. George ran after them, loving being free to run around without Nanny to supervise him. They walked in silence, making sure to look along every corridor.

'What's down there?' asked Lupo. He was sure he saw a shadow. 'I think I just saw something down there.' His whole body was pointing towards a door at the far end of the corridor.

'I'm not sure,' answered Kitty. 'That door is always locked because this corridor is where they store all the old exhibits. The palace had a nice one a while ago with lots of dresses. It was a bit spooky, mind you.' Just then, something caught Kitty's eye. 'Hang on, you're right. There *is* something down there. I just saw a shadow. Come on – let's check it out.'

George got to the door first. He reached up and turned the doorknob. Much to Kitty's surprise, the door opened easily. The three explorers stepped inside slowly. 'Can you see it?' asked Kitty.

'No, maybe it's hiding?' whispered Lupo. The

room was full of things that looked like they belonged in a museum. They took it in turns to look into glass cabinets and boxes filled with fascinating objects. 'We haven't looked over there,' said Lupo. 'Is that a PIRATE SHIP!'

George ran over to a large model pirate ship and screamed, wild with excitement. But Lupo and Kitty didn't move because standing behind the model was the ghost in the black hat. He stood staring down at the ship, looking very unhappy.

Kitty's long tabby tail flicked nervously. 'I don't like it,' she meowed. 'Why is it staring at that ship?'

Lupo spoke as quietly as he could so as not to disturb the sad ghost. 'I don't know. Maybe we should ask it what it's doing up here?'

'You talk to it, if you like. I won't. If you ask me, it's creepy,' she said, swatting Lupo on the back with her tail. 'I doubt you'll get any sense out of it.'

Lupo bravely stepped forwards so that he was at George's side. 'Hello, can I help you? Are you lost, sir?' he asked.

'I'm not lost. But my ship is. I heard that it was here,' replied the friendly but miserable ghost. 'I have been searching for it for a very long time. I have

searched the world
looking for her.'

Lupo wanted to
help. 'I'm sorry, sir, there are
no pirate ships in Kensington Palace.'

The ghost was upset. 'The *Golden Hind* is not a
PIRATE SHIP! It was the proudest ship in Queen
Elizabeth I's Armada. I won't hear of it being called a
PIRATE SHIP!'

Kitty stepped forwards. 'He didn't mean to upset
you, Captain. We just don't understand why you
would think that your ship would be here at
Kensington Palace?'

'PIRATE SHIP!' shouted George. Lupo blushed
and tried to steer George away from the unhappy
spirit.

'What does your ship look like?' Kitty asked. 'Is it
like the model?'

The ghost reached forward and stuck out his
hand. 'Yes this *is* a model of my ship, the *Golden
Hind*, and that is my dog. I miss her and I want to
find her.'

Kitty and Lupo followed the grey misty hand of
the ghost to a point at the end of the boat. Standing

11

on the edge of the boat was a dog. A shaggy grey dog.

'It's a lurcher,' Lupo said confidently, 'so you are looking for your dog, not the ship!'

'That is correct. I am Sir Francis Drake; I sailed the world with my dog. Her name was Whisper and she was the best dog any man could ever have.'

Kitty sashayed around the room. 'At least it's not a lost *Labrador*,' she said with a shudder. 'Walking dustbins, if you ask me. All those things seem to do is eat, slobber and knock things over.'

Lupo was confused. 'How did you lose your dog, Sir Francis?'

The ghostly Sir Francis hung his head low and said, 'I left her with my ship. She was guarding it and protecting the treasure.'

Kitty was half listening and half inspecting her long claws. They were badly in need of a good filing. She would have to 'borrow' one of the Duchess's nail files. She stopped thinking about her nails for a moment and said, 'Did you just say *treasure*?'

'Yes,' answered the ghost in his big black hat, 'and it's cursed treasure. Too dangerous for the likes of men to protect. That is why I left Whisper in charge.'

George was running back and forth around the

ghost, finding it all very funny. 'HAT!' he cried, reaching up for the captain's hat. The captain joined in. He took off his hat and playfully put it on to George's head. 'I'm a PIRATE!' shouted the little prince happily.

Lupo looked at the model of the ship and then turned to Kitty. 'We have to find the ship. If it's here at the palace we can at least try looking for it.' Then he walked towards Sir Francis and said, 'We will help you find your dog, Sir Francis. If Whisper is here, we'll find her.'

Nanny was calling out, 'LUPO!' and then they all heard her say, 'GEORGE, WHERE ARE YOU?'

Kitty grabbed the royal dog and George and pulled them both out of the room, leaving Sir Francis and the model of the *Golden Hind* behind. 'This way! Quick!'

Herbert was in a very good mood. As the Head of Mice Intelligence Section 5, he had access to all sorts of wonderful information. Today he had been given advanced notice of an impending storm. This meant that he had plenty of time to get everyone prepared well ahead.

Just knowing that all the animals had received an alert made him feel better. Now all he needed to do was stock up on iced buns, dust off his books and settle into his office to wait until the storm had passed. Secretly he was looking forward to a few days of peace and quiet. It had been very busy recently. Lupo's adventures – on top of his daily routine – had left him completely exhausted.

Finally, everything was calm. Soon it would be very quiet because the Duke and Duchess had decided to move the family to Norfolk. The Duke was going to work on helicopters. It meant that Lupo wouldn't be based at Kensington Palace any more and, for now, Herbert and his team of agents could relax, safe in the knowledge that the royal dog couldn't get into any trouble. Besides, there was so much work to be caught up on, he doubted whether he would even get a chance to miss the friendly spaniel.

Issy, a sassy mouse from Mice Communications, knocked at Herbert's door, disturbing his thoughts. She was quite the prettiest mouse he had ever seen. She was a rare ginger colour and she had the biggest, happiest smile. Herbert kept his feelings for her a secret but the truth was that he had fallen very much in love with her some years ago. Sadly he never quite got up the courage to talk to her outside of work. He fumbled his words around her, and today was no exception.

'Errr . . . yes . . . um . . . my . . . my . . . Issy,' he tried, blushing from the tips of his long brown ears to the bottom of his long furry tail. 'How may I be of assistance?'

Issy smiled, revealing her pearly white teeth. 'Good afternoon, Herbert. I am not disturbing you, am I? I just had a message for you.' She flicked a tuft of ginger fur out of her eyes. 'I can come back if you're busy.'

'NO!' shouted Herbert a little too loudly. 'I mean no, of course I am not busy at all.'

Issy made herself comfortable in an armchair near his desk. She was careful not to knock anything over. The whole office looked like it could do with a good sort out. It was filled to bursting with reports, files, newspaper pictures, cups of cold tea and the faintest trail of cat smell. 'I was going over the reports from Kensington Palace and I found something rather interesting.'

Herbert was completely bewitched. 'OK, good.'

Issy opened the slim file she was holding. 'A new ghost. I believe it to be Sir Francis Drake. He's at the palace looking for something.'

Herbert snapped awake, determined to invite her out for tea. This was his chance. 'Oh yes, I heard. It's nothing, just another lost ghost. Tell me, are you free for a . . .' But before he could finish she was up and out of her chair.

'You are quite mistaken! I think he could be the key to uncovering a great mystery! Herbert, you are going to want to hear what I have to say about it!'

Issy had never shouted at him before. He found that he couldn't speak, he was so shocked. Issy's mop of ginger fur was flopping around and she stomped about his office. 'Hang on, were you trying to ask me out? Because if you were I'd be delighted to go with you.' Herbert's face lit up for a moment then Issy said, 'It will give us a chance to discuss the lost *Golden Hind* and figure out exactly why that ghost is lurking around Kensington Palace!'

2
The Map

Ebony didn't walk like a normal cat. She didn't sit like a normal cat. In fact, she looked nothing like your average cat. She was bigger, her black fur was softer than regular cats' fur and she walked more gracefully. Her eyes were a glimmering emerald green and when she sat down she took her time, as if she was making herself comfortable on a throne. She had woken up in Buckingham Palace from a hundred-year sleep and then cursed the entire palace. Lupo and his friends had only just managed to stop her from taking over completely. Awake but without anywhere to reign, she had to settle into a very uncomfortable new way of life.

Getting used to modern London itself had not been easy. England's buzzing first city was nothing like her home in ancient Egypt. Being the Queen of the Nile one day then being a litter picker the next was not exactly an easy transition. Living with a smelly old grey cat called Matilda in the royal stables had been no fun, either. Ebony was forced to a sleep amongst hay, lazy horses and flies.

Eventually the stable grew tired of her moaning and she was kicked out. It hadn't been such a bad thing. At least she was now free to roam around the streets of London and her fur didn't pong of horses.

Late at night she saw London come alive with other unhappy creatures who relished her stories of plenty. They also craved her old way of life. They, like her, wanted to live in a world where animals ruled not humans. But if she had known that trying to steal a throne would lead to such a miserable life, she might have thought twice about waking up in this century.

Every time she walked past the gates to Buckingham Palace, she was reminded how close she had come to getting back her throne. She also thought of her most powerful ally, Vulcan the royal dorgi.

In the cold dawn, as the sunlight spilt across London, she'd imagine Vulcan asleep in the royal bedroom, uncomfortable in his gilded cage, waiting for the perfect moment to take over Buckingham Palace. Even Vulcan didn't see he was a prisoner to the humans' Queen. Vulcan, like her, was thirsting for animal freedom – she had seen it in his eyes – but she didn't trust him. He was a wickedly evil dog. Even so, she knew befriending him was the key to them both getting what they wanted.

Ebony slipped effortlessly in and out of the royal gates early every morning, teasing the guards as they shooed her away. Creeping away from the light of the famous palace she would follow the same path. Daily, the cunning cat made her way past the palace and up to the tube station near St James's Park.

She had a very important friend living at Green Park Station. His name was Harold and he was a very old and lonely homeless man. He spoke in a tone that suggested he had once been important. He and Ebony had much in common. Like Ebony, he spent most of his nights walking the streets – staring up at the house he had once lived in. They were both unable to forget the past. He liked to take care of her and he was the first human in almost 10,000 years she trusted. Every morning she ran to see him and he would feed her the fresh milk he was given from the back door of the Ritz hotel.

Ebony was fiercely protective of Harold. He had no one to talk to but her, because she scared off kindly, helpful strangers who only wanted to help him. He didn't mind that she was so difficult. He called her Queenie, which amused her – if only she could tell him where she had really come from! Every now and then he tried to pick her up and give her a cuddle but she was wise to human ways and was careful never getting too close.

When the weather was bad, Harold gave her a warm, dry home in a shopping trolley in the undergrowth. He shared the food he was given by passersby and when everyone went back to their homes, he would tell her stories about the beautiful world he had once lived in.

Apart from the clothes on his back and the shopping cart, Harold had just one other thing, which he kept close to his chest. Ebony, of course, noticed it and her curiosity was getting stronger and stronger. She wanted it, whatever it was. Every now and then, he would tap his chest to check that 'it' had not gone.

On one particular morning, she woke to find Harold quite unwell. Winter in the royal park had been unforgiving. Through his raspy cough he had reached into his old coat and removed a carefully folded bit of leather and paper. 'Here, Queenie, come and see this,' Harold said, wheezing on the cold ground.

She wrapped herself around his shoulders and pawed at the piece of paper and leather, trying to get a better look at it.

'Now, Queenie, be very careful,' he warned. 'This is a map. It is my most treasured possession. I found it in the basement of the British Museum. I believe it is a treasure map. I have tried to find the treasure many times but have always failed. The treasure lies beyond my reach.' He began coughing hard. 'But not yours. I want you to have it. You must carry on. Find the treasure and have a better life.'

She stayed with him until he stopped coughing and fell into an endless sleep. Then she pulled the map from his cold hands and ran away, never stopping to look back.

The map was hers now.

Vulcan had managed to sneak out of the palace. Being a small dog meant that it was easy to disappear, and over the years he had perfected various escape routes. It was a very different way of life in the City of Creatures beneath Buckingham Palace. He had to be extra careful, because he couldn't afford to be seen down here. There were more than a few creatures that would want to swap places with him.

As he walked into the noisy hustle and bustle of the famous animal city, he dropped his gaze, careful not to catch anyone's eyes. The city's creatures swamped the shops and food areas. It was alive with stray dogs and cats, and foxes, as well as lots and lots of rats – and all of them would kill him for a night in the comfort of Buckingham Palace's kitchens.

A while ago a little boy discovered the underground city, but for all his chatter no one bothered to come down and see it for themselves. This was a city created for the abandoned, lost and unloved. The animals that sought shelter here rarely left, so they began their families here, and those families had other families and so the strange animal city grew and grew. It was no place for a refined dog, let alone a royal one.

He'd met dogs living amongst the humans that shunned any talk of squalor. Like him they enjoyed their two meals a day, lolling around on overstuffed sofas and being allowed to play in the lush homes of their owners. Belonging to someone was no bad thing for most dogs, but Vulcan was different – he detested being led anywhere by anyone. He neither fitted up in the palace nor down in the animal city. The world he created in his mind was somewhere where animals like him could roam freely above ground, undisturbed by the humans, and he remained hell bent on trying to get it all the way he wanted it.

So far, all his attempts had been thwarted by the Duke and Duchess's cocker spaniel Lupo. The public adored Prince George's brown-eyed best friend with his wagging, feathery tail and happy smiling face. But

Vulcan detested him. Annoyingly, Holly, the Queen's favourite corgi, had grown very fond of Lupo. But Lupo and Holly were nothing without Kitty the Kensington Palace stray tabby, and that troublesome mouse, Herbert. The cat, in Vulcan's opinion, belonged amongst the forgotten underground. Herbert the mouse had managed to single-handedly train Lupo from being a simple farm dog into today's national hero. Together these four friends had stopped all Vulcan's grandest plans to take over the throne of England. Thankfully, their run of 'luck' was about to end.

It had been while reading an old book from the library at Buckingham Palace that Vulcan discovered a forgotten mystery that he was determined to solve. The dusty tome contained a story about a missing Tudor ship called the *Golden Hind*. It had been lost and, perfectly for him, it was filled to bursting with gold and treasure.

Vulcan's plan was simple: find the *Golden Hind* and use the treasure to create the animal city of his

dreams. No longer would creatures have to skulk around in the slums of the city beneath Buckingham

Palace. He would build them an empire.

Unfortunately, there was one snag he had to iron out. He couldn't find the *Golden Hind* alone. For a plan of this size, he needed help and there was only one creature in the kingdom that detested Lupo as much as he did, and, better still, had a crew of her own that would work for nothing. Ebony.

Vulcan had followed the ancient Egyptian cat's new life with interest. He knew there were two things that Ebony disliked most in this century. They were Lupo and chewing gum. Like chewing gum, the royal spaniel also seemed to be everywhere and whenever she saw a picture of him or heard someone mention his name her green eyes glowed. Vulcan knew that, deep inside, Ebony had vowed to get her revenge, and she also wanted to make the Duke and Duchess's dog pay for ruining her plans to curse Buckingham Palace.

Claw, the snivelling buck rat who worked for Edgar the raven – the master of the Tower of London – had been forced to arrange tonight's meeting between Vulcan and Ebony in the City of Creatures. Vulcan had caught the rat in the palace kitchens again, Claw had told him that Ebony had acquired a 'treasure map'. Vulcan listened with interest as Claw explained that Ebony had taken the map to the Crocodile King beneath the River Thames. The King had invested two large beasts in helping with the discovery of a missing ship. Vulcan knew it had to be a map that would take him to the *Golden Hind*.

The bad royal corgi had to get his hands on the map and take command of Ebony's hapless crew of creatures. But first he needed to convince the Egyptian cat that if they worked together to find the treasure, they could both get their revenge on Lupo and his friends.

Vulcan was hiding beneath an oversized cape. The hood was lifted over his slim head and his face poked out just far enough for him to see where he was going. Underneath it, his little dorgi body twitched with discomfort. He ran his long pink tongue over his whiskers and his beady eyes searched out the Katz Bar. His destination was near a large marketplace. He trotted faster, keen to hurry his business and return to the palace.

A clock badly tacked to the City's Town Hall showed that it was almost breakfast time. Vulcan thought of the chef at the palace who would be just getting started on the Queen's bacon. The palace staff would be looking for him soon. Wherever he slipped off to, he always had to make sure he was back in time for breakfast. These days no one seemed to notice his comings and goings but the Queen would notice if he missed breakfast time.

4

Sir Francis's Model Ship

After all the trouble they had caused exploring, Lupo, Kitty and George were being made to spend the rest of the afternoon in the kitchen. Lupo listened to the radio blasting out warnings of an impending storm. Much to his amusement, ever since news of the troublesome storm had been announced, Kitty had taken to hiding in a cupboard near the cornflakes. There was nothing she detested more than the great outdoors. Lupo loved to go on long, wet and windy walks with lots of muddy puddles and end the day with a good long sleep by the fireside, whilst Kitty preferred to snuggle up in the Duke's brother's pillows in Apartment 2.

The Duchess was baking a cake for tea with the Queen. She was far too busy to notice the stormy weather. The only thing that distracted her from her eggs and buttercream was a loud bang coming from upstairs. 'I hope the Duke will be down soon. The Queen will be here shortly and he's been upstairs cleaning out that room all afternoon!' she muttered to Lupo.

Lupo thought about Sir Francis's shaggy dog. Kitty was refusing to help him search for the missing animal and he could hear the Duke moving heavy boxes around upstairs. He wondered if Sir Francis was still haunting the model of the *Golden Hind*, yearning for his lost dog.

The Queen and her corgis were expected for teatime. So Holly would be here soon, too, and Lupo hoped that she might want to join him in searching for Whisper, the pirate dog. The thought of having Holly around filled him with joy. Only he couldn't understand why, whenever he saw her, his stomach leapt into his throat and his heart beat faster. He put it down to the corgi being so pretty; that and her perfect blue eyes.

The Duke walked into the room with a large clipboard. 'That's nearly all of it. I think I have gone through every box and I have found some pretty incredible pieces. No wonder George and Lupo were up there – it's more like a museum than a storeroom. Would you believe that I even found a model of a missing English ship.'

The Duchess smiled. 'Are you talking about the *Golden Hind*?'

'Yes, that's it!' The Duke returned, holding the large model. 'It's quite something. We must arrange for it to be taken care of. I'm not sure it belongs with us in Norfolk and it certainly shouldn't be hidden away.'

Lupo ran around the model but there was no sign of Sir Francis Drake's ghost. George cried out, wanting another look at the ship.

'I think I will put it in the nursery for now,' said the Duke. 'On the bookshelf so that George can look at it.' When he returned, he said, 'Something smells good. I could smell it all the way down the corridor. Is it a chocolate cake?'

'Yes, I've made it for our afternoon tea,' the Duchess said. She gave her husband some soft buttercream on a spoon, and looked out of the kitchen window. 'I hope that ship will be all right in the nursery. I would hate for anything to happen to it.'

The Duke smiled. 'Hmmmm. Lovely chocolate buttercream, my favourite!'

Looking out the window, the Duchess could see and hear the rain. 'That storm is coming in. Just look at that extreme weather!'

Lupo jumped up and stood next to the Duchess. Cleverly, he balanced on his hind legs. Out of the window, he could see the security men being blown around by the stormy wind. He had never seen so many leaves in the air.

The Duke sounded concerned. 'Gosh, you're right. The weather is starting to get really bad.'

Just then, a huge gust of wind blew open the windows above the sink. The little latch banged.

The noise succeeded in attracting Kitty's attention. She poked her head out of her cupboard and watched the humans. She meowed and said, 'I'm telling you, Lupo. That storm is going to get *much* worse. We cats have a nose for storms.'

'Let's leave the cake to cool and go and have a look at Daddy's ship!' said the Duchess to the royal children. She took her cake out of the oven and put it into the pantry to cool. Then the entire family followed the Duke to the nursery.

Kitty waited until the humans had gone before emerging from the safety of the cupboard. 'Is the coast clear?' she asked.

'Yes, they have all gone,' Lupo answered.

Kitty shook her head. '*Coast* clear. Do you get it? Err . . . life at sea. You see, I haven't forgotten about the ghost or his missing dog! I couldn't imagine anything so bad. Nope, I'm quite happy here in our little palace.' Kitty tutted, then she said, 'You won't be going looking for that dog down in the City of Creatures, that's for sure. With all this wind and rain, I expect it will be getting very crowded with animals seeking shelter.'

Lupo had always wanted to explore the animal city. 'Do you really think Whisper could be down there?' Kitty shrugged, unsure of how to answer, but Lupo felt an adventure coming on. He asked, 'Will you come and look for her? If she *is* down in the City and we find her, we could make that sad ghost very happy.'

Kitty shook her head. '*No!* I am not getting involved in another one of your crazy adventures, Lupo. I am not searching for some old dog and I'm certainly not taking you down to the sewers. It's not the place for a royal dog. So no, and no again, and no once more!'

Lupo sat on the kitchen floor, staring up at Kitty who had made herself comfortable on the kitchen top. She began playing with the Duchess's priceless blue engagement ring, which had been left near the sink.

Lupo wasn't about to give in. 'Who said anything about an adventure? I would hardly say following a few pipes down to the city is a major expedition. We can take Holly with us! What else have we got to do this afternoon?'

Kitty lay flat on the worktop and stuck both paws in her ears. 'That's exactly what you said the last time, when we had to go and find the crown jewels! I AM NOT LISTENING TO YOU!'

Lupo barked. 'KITTY, LOOK! HE'S BACK!'

Standing in the corner of the kitchen was the spirit of Sir Francis Drake.

'I overheard you talking,' the ghost began. 'Do you really think you could try and find her? Only I'd be happy to help. I have a few clues and I think I have finally figured out a way through the maze.'

Kitty stuck her head over the counter so that she

was peering into Lupo's face. 'So there are clues? And a maze? THIS *IS* STARTING TO SOUND LIKE AN ADVENTURE, LUPO!!' She rolled on to her back, exposing her long tabby belly. 'Look, Sir Francis Drake, please stop encouraging Lupo! He can't go and find your dog! It's quite impossible.' Then she slid over to the side of the worktop and dangled her paws into the sink. 'It's out of the question entirely!'

Lupo's black tail was wagging helplessly behind him, a sure sign of his eagerness to explore, and his long velvety black ears stood alert, ready to listen to the ghostly instructions. 'AND stop wagging that tail!' she cried.

'Humans found the maze impossible, but there *is* a way through,' said Sir Francis. 'You are animals, so I'm sure you would find it much easier.'

Kitty sighed. 'Well, if you think you know the way, why don't you go yourself – you don't need us!'

Lupo didn't like Kitty being so rude to their guest, even if he was a ghost. 'Kitty! I promised Sir Francis I would help him to find his dog.'

The ghost glided across the room and stopped at the pantry door. He bent to smell the delicious chocolate cake. 'You see, I am just a ghost these days.

I lack the strength and courage I used to have. You will need to go down to your City of Creatures. I believe the fastest route is that way,' he said, pointing at the secret entrance hidden at the back of the pantry that led down to the Red route. He mused, 'Those secret animal passages are fascinating. You animals really are terribly clever. I shall look forward to assisting you on your adventure, Master Lupo. I am sure it will be like the old days, when I would sail out into the big ocean looking for new lands.'

Kitty grumbled, 'Yes, it sounds exactly like that . . . NOT!'

Lupo tried begging. 'Kitty, please. He needs us and I've been looking for a reason to go and explore the famous city. This might be my last chance before I have to move to Norfolk with the family.'

'NO,' said Kitty, kicking open the bread bin.

'What do you mean, NO?' sniffed Lupo.

'Just because the family is going away for a while, doesn't mean that you can just run amok willy-nilly. Have you lost every last one of your dog brain cells?'

Lupo looked blankly at the palace cat, unsure of what the problem was. Kitty rolled her eyes and tried to explain. 'It wouldn't just be the storm we would have to worry about, it's all those cats. They'd love to get their claws into a royal dog. Especially since you set that awful Ebony free. I wasn't going to tell you, but I think you need to know: that ancient cat has stirred up a whole lot of troublesome cats and she's even got her own gang now!'

Kitty leapt down from the kitchen top and began pacing around the kitchen. Her long tail curled around Lupo as she walked.

Kitty sighed. 'Ebony just couldn't go quietly, could she? I heard she has a lizard and a crocodile in her gang these days. Mighty dangerous. I'm telling you, black cats are nothing but trouble, no matter how old they are.'

'Ebony is in the City of Creatures?' said Lupo.

'Yes, as a matter of fact she's taken over the Katz Bar.' Kitty sat down, determined not to move an inch. 'I couldn't help you even if I wanted to. I've got far too much to do today,' she said, ignoring Lupo's pleading eyes. 'I'm planning on spending the afternoon in the laundry room, where it's warm, dry and there is no maze or storm or any dreadful crocodiles to chase me around.'

Sir Francis had heard enough. He floated towards the back door, a tear rolling down his cheek. Lupo watched as the ghost looked out at the wind and the rain, and then disappeared through the back door, leaving the palace creatures alone once more.

'And good riddance!' humphed Kitty.

Outside, the storm was gathering strength. Dark clouds hung all around the palace. Lupo walked down the long, empty corridors of the apartment. He could hear the trees in the park outside bending and cracking. The wind was screeching around the palace's red brickwork. He joined the ghosts of King William and Queen Mary as they hovered at the window watching Sir Francis, who was pointing to the weathervane on the roof.

The kindly King William cleared his throat. 'Just look at that ghost down there. Poor Sir Francis. He was such a terrific explorer. Mary, did you know he discovered the Americas? He was a legend when he was alive and now look at him, moping. I'll never understand why he insists on standing outside the palace when the weather is stormy.' King William twisted his curly hair between his fingers.

The beautiful but ghostly Queen Mary nodded in agreement. 'I tried going out one time – it was simply dreadful. I really can't recommend it, Your Royal Highness. Ghosts don't do very well in wind. Just look at Sir Francis down there – the poor thing will catch his death all over again. What good will it do?'

'Mary, did you know he captured most of the Spanish fleet and all their gold! Such a shame the *Golden Hind* is now lost. If you ask me I don't think he ever got over the loss of that dog of his.'

Lupo watched as King William's ghost tried knocking on the windowpane, but his lacy sleeve kept floating right through it. The King grew bored with trying to get Sir Francis's attention, and he gave up.

William sighed heavily. 'I think we'd better retire early, Mary, and resume our haunting tomorrow. No tourists will come today. No one to frighten.'

Mary nodded in agreement and Lupo watched as they both made their excuses and floated away.

A short while later the large housekeeper screamed and ran past shouting, 'GHOSTS! I'VE JUST SEEN GHOSTS!'

Lupo giggled behind his paw but stopped when he heard a familiar voice. Herbert was standing with his hands on his hips, shaking his head. 'I've told you it's just not funny. That's another housekeeper the palace will lose. I must have a word with those two ghosts. Honestly, they float around here day and night menacing everyone and for what? A few laughs?' Herbert sighed. 'Lupo, what on earth are you doing just sitting here anyway?'

'Hi, Herbert, I was just looking at the storm.'

The Head of Mice Intelligence Section 5 clambered up on to the spaniel's neck, and then crawled on to his head. Now, like Lupo, he could see out of the main window. At this time of day, Percy the pigeon was normally found to be sitting on top Queen Victoria's head but today he was nowhere in sight. Instead, Herbert could see visitors and staff wrestling with their umbrellas, trying desperately to get home. He watched them struggling.

'My reports say that this is only the beginning. The main storm is expected to hit later,' Herbert grumbled.

40

Lupo groaned. At least he'd had a walk earlier. 'Herbert, why is Sir Francis Drake still outside?'

Herbert ran along Lupo's whiskers to get a better look at the angry ghost outside the palace. 'Issy told me he was here. It's said that when he returned to England with the *Golden Hind*, it was filled to bursting with Spanish gold. But the ship went missing during a big storm – although its weathervane is now on top of this very palace. We've never had the chance to interview him. I have sent many agents on the case, but he just mumbles, *"Whisper, such a loyal companion. I'll find the Hind. I'll never stop searching to find you."*'

'Whisper was his dog,' said Lupo. 'He told me. Is that why you are here? Have you come to help Kitty and me find Sir Francis's ship?'

Herbert nodded. 'Indeed, that is exactly why I have come. I had a most enjoyable cup of tea with Miss Issy in Mice Communications. She is adamant that the *Golden Hind* is somewhere here at Kensington Palace. I suggest we get to work immediately. Issy came up with some clever ideas about where the ship and the dog might be . . .' Lupo could see Herbert's cheeks blush, a sure sign that he really did like Issy very much. Herbert knocked the side of his head with his paw. 'Sorry, I was somewhere else for a moment. Lovely Issy . . . oh sorry again . . . so yes, erm.'

A lightning bolt hit the roof of the palace, filling the corridor with a flash, followed by a rumble of thunder. They both jumped at the terrible noise. Lupo watched as several squirrels dived for cover next to a tree in the palace gardens. 'Those poor animals. Kitty says they retreat to the City of Creatures when it gets bad like this.'

Herbert nodded. 'The City of Creatures does get very busy. But it's fine just as long as it doesn't flood.'

With the noise of the storm ringing in his ears, Lupo fell quiet. He felt suddenly very concerned. 'Herbert, what if it does flood? Will all those animals be all right? There is plenty of shelter in the palace basement. Do you think we could let some in. Just for the night?'

Herbert was reminded of how thoughtful the royal dog was. 'I'm afraid not. We can't compromise the palace. There is plenty of shelter in the city. The animals have had lots of time to get prepared. Don't worry yourself.'

As they made their way to the kitchen, Bernie appeared in the corridor in front of them. He looked gravely concerned. 'Herbert, Lupo, excuse me. Might I have a word?'

Both animals rushed to the mouse's side. Lupo asked, 'What is it, Bernie? What's wrong?'

'It's the city, Herbert. It's flooding. The animals down there need you to come quickly.'

Herbert was shocked. He looked at Bernie and nodded, 'Oh dear. That is not good. I'd better go straight away. Lupo, I'll report back when I can. I'm sorry, our hunt for the *Golden Hind* and Whisper the dog must wait.'

5

A Mystery

Holly sat on the Queen's lap on the short journey to Kensington Palace. Willow and Monty were happy beside Candy in the other seat. The Queen was looking forward to an afternoon with her family, even though the weather was dreadful.

'Well, dogs,' Her Majesty said. 'The Duke tells me that the Duchess has made a splendid chocolate cake for tea! I do love cake. I know that they are very much looking forward to having us so you all must all be on your best behaviour.' She glanced down at Vulcan who was flicking the tassels on the rug that covered the royal legs. 'That means no trouble, Vulcan. Everyone has their hands full with this storm. To think of all those grand old oaks falling — it breaks my heart. I just hope that Windsor Castle hasn't suffered too much. Holly, we must check that the horses are fine. You know how much Burmese hates stormy weather.'

Vulcan tuned out. He wasn't in the least bit concerned about Windsor or, for that matter, about visiting Kensington Palace. As the Queen continued to talk about her fears and worries, he hopped up and gazed out of the window. The storm was lashing out, much like his mood.

At least his meeting with Ebony at the Katz Bar had proved to be invaluable. The fact that she had already discovered a map leading to the location of the lost ship was a stroke of good luck. Ebony had boasted that she had traded for it in the city's market. Vulcan knew she was lying.

As the car swung through the gates and on to the long private driveway leading to Kensington Palace he sat back down. First chance he had to get away he'd be down to the city and in search of the cat's map.

Lupo was waiting for Holly at the door. When she arrived she could immediately tell something was wrong. Instead of greeting her in his usual way, today his tail didn't move, his eyes shone with concern and his ears hung that little bit lower, and heavier.

Thankfully, the Duke and Duchess were far more gracious with their welcome. All the palace staff had lined up inside and, as the door opened and Her Majesty stepped into the palace, they all bowed and curtseyed.

Holly followed Her Majesty as she took her time to shake hands and have a warm moment with everyone.

'Welcome to Kensington Palace,' said the Duchess. 'We are so pleased you could come.'

The royal dogs trotted behind the Queen as the Duke and Duchess took her for tea in the small drawing room. Holly was able to spend some time with Lupo. 'And there was I thinking you would be happy to see me.' Holly bustled ahead of the spaniel and into the central hallway. 'Come on, take me to the nursery and tell me everything that's bothering you. Those soppy eyes don't fool me for one moment.'

Kitty was woken by Lupo and Holly banging on the laundry room door. 'Kitty, are you in there?' they asked. She tried to ignore them by burying her head amongst Princess Charlotte's clean dresses. 'Kitty, please, come out. We are worried about Herbert.'

One swift kick of her back leg and the door to the cupboard swung open. 'Let me get this straight. You are worried about a highly skilled mouse? Herbert is more than capable of taking care of himself. He's probably in his office, munching on some soft cheese with a cute lady mouse.'

Lupo shook his head. 'I don't think so. He went down to the City of Creatures. They needed him; it was something about a flood. We found some mice in the upstairs rooms. They've told us that the City of Creatures has been practically washed away.'

Kitty carefully pawed her way out of the warm basket. She prided herself on her stealth capabilities. 'Those mice have runs that can get anywhere these days – they have their own network. I'm sure he is fine. This is Herbert we're talking about! As for the animals – I can assure you both, the city is big enough for all kinds of creatures. Even if it's flooding.' The palace tabby began licking herself clean. 'Don't suppose you have seen the Buckingham Palace chef yet? I hear he's cooking up a large salmon tonight. I'm starving,' Kitty said with a yawn.

Lupo did something he was sure he'd regret in the future. He grabbed Kitty's paw and yanked her to the pantry. The palace cat was not happy about being dragged anywhere. Several spiders watched as the royal pets argued.

'YOUUUUCHHHHH . . . stop it!' she meowed. 'LUPO, what on earth has got into you today?'

Only when they were all safely tucked away into the cupboard did he speak. 'Herbert went this way. Come on. We are all going to the City of Creatures. NOW!'

Kitty paused to think of a way to put a stop to Lupo's attempts to leave. In the end she said, 'No, we are not. Are we, Holly?'

Holly had been watching everything unfold. Deep down she knew Lupo was right but she also knew that it was an impossible task. 'Kitty's right. What can we do even if we do get down to the city?'

Lupo looked into friends' eyes. 'I thought you both would understand. Herbert is our friend. All right, we'll wait until we hear something from him.'

Happy that she had won, Kitty pushed open the pantry door and headed in the direction of the main kitchens. With the storm raging, the Queen had decided to stay for dinner. A sumptuous feast was being prepared, which included some of the best Scottish salmon.

The palace tabby looked over her shoulder as she walked away from Lupo. He was still sitting alone in the pantry surrounded by spiders. 'And as for that ghost's dog. It's long gone. Forget about it!'

Holly had her paw on Lupo's shoulder. 'We are royal dogs. We can't just disappear today – the Queen is here. We need to wait for news. I'm sure Herbert will be all right. Now, why don't you tell me about the ghost and his dog?'

6

Lost Secrets Revealed

The quickest route to the city was down the secret animal passage known as the Red route. On his way through the pantry, Herbert had stopped to say a brief hello to the spider family and had collected some crumbs from the Duchess's chocolate cake. The spiders watched as he had sent instructions with Bernie to MI5 HQ. All agents were to assist with clearing any blocked ways in and out of the parks.

The spiders remarked that it was a pleasure having such an important mouse using the Red route. They had told him that many animals had done an excellent job cleaning and sprucing up the route recently and that the Kensington Palace mice had been joined by those from Buckingham Palace, Sandringham and even Balmoral, working together to restore every inch of the secret animal passage. Even the lamp-lighting sparrows had assisted in cleaning and repairing the delicately carved ceiling, which served as a map for creatures looking to get to other royal residences.

Herbert wanted to hurry but he was never not polite. So he said his goodbyes and promised to return soon. Then he ran as fast as his furry little paws could take him until he was stopped by a mouse called Tommy, one of his field agents who had been assigned to restoration duties along the route.

Tommy knocked right into Herbert as he swung from a long bit of gold thread attached to an old tapestry on the wall. 'Sorry, sir,' Tommy said. 'Won't be a moment, then I'll have this thing out of your way.'

Herbert waited while Tommy stitched the long bit of thread into the tapestry. Tommy was working on a Tudor design, which meant that it must have been created while the Tudor royal family ruled all of England and Wales. It was dated from 1485 to 1603. Herbert was impressed: the priceless piece of art could have been presented to any one of the Tudor Kings or Queens, which included the great King

Henry VIII and Queen Elizabeth I. Somehow, it had found its way down to the secret animal passage.

Tommy apologised. 'All done. Sorry if I got in your way, sir.'

'No apologies necessary, Tommy,' Herbert said. 'The Tudors would have been proud of the work you have done repairing one of their great artworks.'

Tommy was delighted that the famous Head of MI5 had stopped to notice his hard work. 'Thank you, sir. Yes, it's quite something. Who would have thought that at the same time this was being created, Henry VIII had six wives, Sir Francis Drake sailed the high seas and William Shakespeare's words wooed the great Queen Elizabeth I. It must have been quite something to be a mouse back in Tudor times.'

Herbert looked more closely at the tapestry. Carefully stitched on to the large canvas was a golden ship, shimmering in yellow sunlight. It looked mighty and proud as it sailed on a cotton sea of blue and green thread. On board, sailors were celebrating and on the shore people were cheering. He could also see a grey dog standing on the deck of the ship next to the captain with a young boy. A queen was waving as the mighty ship headed towards her. Behind her, sewn on to some flags, were the Tudor roses.

'Sir Francis Drake . . . hmmm . . .' Herbert said. 'Now that is a coincidence – that's the *Golden Hind*.'

Tommy smiled. 'Indeed it could be, sir, the famous *Golden Hind*. It's a shame that it's lost. Legend has it that it was hidden away, to protect its treasure from thieves.'

Herbert laughed. 'You are quite right, the treasure on board was said to be enough to drive any sailor mad with gold fever.'

It was the dog on the tapestry – which stood so regal and proud – that snapped him out of his daydreams. It reminded him of Lupo. Herbert also thought of Sir Francis's lost dog. It must have sailed on the high seas, protecting the ship's captain just as Lupo loyally took care of his family. The dog was not a spaniel, but a grey lurcher. Herbert could imagine the dog barking orders at the ship's rats as they dived for cover.

'A pirate dog!' he blurted unintentionally.

'Quite right! A pirate dog!' said Tommy. 'I should be finished tomorrow. Nice to see that someone appreciates all my efforts.'

Herbert nodded and reached into his trusty green

cardigan pocket to pull out a couple of crumbs from the Duchess's cake. 'Here, Tommy. Take this. It's awfully tasty. I have more than enough for myself.' He handed half the crumbs to the hard-working agent. 'Right, I'd better be going.'

Tommy handed Herbert a ball of the golden thread. 'Thanks for the cake! In return, take this thread. I have plenty. You never know when it might come in handy.' Herbert tucked the ball into his pocket and thanked the mouse.

Tommy wiped his brow. 'Yes, you'd better be hurrying along, sir. Last time I looked, that storm was getting worse. So you'd better watch out. I can't begin to imagine what kind of state the City of Creatures might be in.'

Herbert waved goodbye and tried to pick up his pace. The city needed him but he wished that he were headed back to his warm dry office to share another cup of tea with the lovely Issy. Thinking of her reminded him that he'd left Lupo in such a hurry, he hadn't shared what the pretty mouse had told him about the strange ghost and the clues around the palace.

The pipe slide Herbert rode down carried him deeper into the animals' city. As he approached the exit he could hear rumbling and animals calling out to each other. He flew out of the slide and landed in a muddy puddle. 'Oh. Oh my, this is not good.'

A large family of foxes was taking shelter with their young near a mole's home. The kindly mole was running backwards and forwards, trying to feed the young cubs that were scrapping over bits of a discarded ham sandwich. The mother looked defeated. It was most unusual to see such a large family this deep in the city – they normally preferred to stay close to the entrances to the parks.

The fox saw Herbert. She thanked the helpful mole for feeding her skittish young cubs then turned to him. 'Herbert, we need you. The route is blocked and the floodwaters are rising. There is nowhere left to turn.'

'Of course, Mrs Fox. Have you considered retreating to Hyde Park?' offered Herbert.

'We've lost the exits to Hyde Park, Green Park and even St James's Park. The mud is moving too quickly. Everyone has moved further down into the city. Herbert, I have seen many storms but nothing as awful as this ever before.'

Pretty soon, Herbert was surrounded by desperate animals, all wanting his help. He ran ahead to see if he could find a way out for everyone. Mrs Fox was right – all the exits to the parks were clogged with debris from the raging storm. Thick mud covered everything. There was no escape for the larger animals. There was, however, a small gap between two large boulders. Bats, small birds, mice and even insects, were carefully picking their way through.

Luckily, Herbert was small enough to squeeze in. He emerged on the other side between some branches that had been washed into the city. At first, he tried walking. Then, as he saw the water rising, he began to run, all the while looking for a way out for the other animals. Eventually, he was jumping from branches and tumbling stones, searching here there and everywhere. He only stopped for a moment to catch his breath. But it wasn't any good. There was no way out.

Herbert took a big breath and tried to calm down. As he did, he realised he was quite lost. The storm had washed away so many of the mice runs through the city that he had no idea where he was.

Standing on the edge of a fast-moving river of mud he sat down, totally exhausted. On the other side of the river, he could see rats, cats and even a crocodile watching as the dirty water picked up speed.

After some time, Herbert picked himself up and carried on walking for what seemed like a very long time, constantly aware of the fear and desperation in the animals' faces. He could only hope that they were not about to lose the city.

He tripped on a branch and found himself sliding into the floodwaters. The slippery mud pulled him in deeper. He fought for air as the animals watching tried to rescue him. Someone threw in a large twig and the last thing he remembered was pulling himself on to it and thinking 'Lupo' before everything went black.

Herbert woke up in a very dark place. There was a chink of yellow light coming from something far away in the distance. He rolled over to find that he was lying next to some very cold hard stone.

Thankfully, his glasses were still on the edge of his long nose. Reaching out with both hands, he checked to see if he had broken anything and was relieved to find that he was in a most acceptable state. Apart from a nasty bump on the side of his head, he was fine. Rubbing the sore bump with his paw, he stood up, happy to be standing on solid ground once more.

He took a moment to clean his glasses and then attempted to work out where he was.

It was a cave. The storm had washed away the mud that had kept it hidden, creating the space he now found himself in. Looking up, he could see the faintest illumination coming from beyond a ring of large stones. 'At least there is light,' he said, staring at the stones. 'How curious.'

The light flickered and Herbert shouted: 'HELLO, IS THERE ANYONE THERE?' And his little voice echoed loudly back. 'I COULD DO WITH A LITTLE HELP. I SEEM TO BE LOST!'

Looking upwards, he could see a soft glow bouncing all around the interior of the cave. 'I CAN SEE YOUR LIGHT! COULD YOU POSSIBLY SHOW ME THE WAY OUT?' But no one replied. 'WHOOO HOOOO!' Herbert cried out. 'HELLO?'

Then the light went out.

In front of Herbert was a very tall stone. It was perfectly cut into a large square. Running along besides it he found another equally large stone, then another and another. He sat down on the floor to have a good think. The stones around him looked like they had been arranged into a large maze.

From the size and shape of the stones he knew that the strange underground structure must have been lost under the mud for some time and, just like the cave that contained it, the storm must have been responsible for revealing it. 'How did a maze get down here?' he wondered.

He ran beyond the stones and came to a pair of large, scary statues. They were enormous stone Minotaurs who appeared to be fighting. The huge hoofed beasts had long horns that clashed together. Herbert dived for cover and said to himself, 'Maybe these two are on guard, warning all who come close. Perhaps this is the entrance to the maze?'

Herbert soon saw that he was right: this was the entrance to the dark labyrinth beyond. For a while he was tempted to go in and explore but then remembered that Mrs Fox and the other animals needed him, so he set about trying to find his way out.

Once he located it, he carefully marked the outside of the nearest tunnel so that he could return. By his calculations, he was almost directly under the Kensington Palace gardens, which meant that the maze had to have a royal connection.

Two badgers and an otter had managed to break through some blocked logs and finally the animals were able to make their way to various shelters around Kensington Gardens and Hyde Park. Mrs Fox and her young cubs thanked Herbert for his efforts in finding them and escorting them to safety. Only when everyone was safe and the magpie police confirmed that everyone was accounted for did he stop to rest and think about the maze.

Someone had gone to a lot of trouble to build it near the City of Creatures. Herbert said to himself, 'It has to protect the *Golden Hind*! It must lie beyond the maze. That is why Sir Francis Drake has come now – he's been waiting for it to be revealed. The storm must have uncovered it! And I'll bet he knows the way through the maze!'

7

A Clue

Lupo had been pacing the nursery ever since they had left the pantry. Holly watched his unease and wished that Herbert would hurry back with some good news – even though it was hard to imagine that there could be much of it. Outside, the storm was battering every windowpane. Inside, the room felt tense.

Everyone was on edge – apart from Kitty who was back from the kitchens and was literally standing on the edge of the large bookcase, blowing raspberries down to Princess Charlotte, who was giggling at the naughty cat. Kitty loved to clown around with the little princess so every now and then, just to make the princess laugh, Kitty would pretend to fall off the bookcase.

Prince George was lying on the floor with his

thumb in his mouth staring up at the ceiling. 'Lupo, when can we go outside and play?' He was bored of having to wait for the storm to pass.

Lupo replied, 'Soon, I hope, George.'

Nanny interrupted them all. 'Now come on, you lot. The Queen is upstairs. I think we should all go and say hello. That includes you, Kitty. Get down from there. This is a nursery not a jungle.'

Kitty began climbing down. She was near to the bottom of the bookcase when she slipped and knocked the precious model of the *Golden Hind* on to the floor. It lay on its side, but something had fallen out of it and Lupo watched as it rolled under the princess's cot.

Nanny rushed over and picked up the model, putting it back on the bookcase. 'You are very lucky it's not broken! Come along, Charlotte and George. And Kitty: NO MORE climbing.'

Lupo waited until Nanny had gone with the children before running under the cot and rescuing what had fallen out of the ship. Kitty and Holly huddled around Lupo to see the tiny dog from the wooden model that was in his hand.

'Whisper, I will never stop looking for you,' came

a voice from the corner of the room. The royal pets all turned round to see that Sir Francis's sad ghost was back. 'I promised her I would return to the *Golden Hind* to free her.'

Kitty yanked the dog away from Lupo. He lunged forwards to grab it back. They pulled at the tiny dog until its leg fell off, revealing a thin roll of paper.

'Kitty, Lupo, you've both found something!' said Holly, carefully unwinding the paper. On it was written: THE *GOLDEN HIND* LIES BEYOND THE MAZE.

'A maze? What's that?' Kitty asked.

Lupo tried to explain. 'It's a kind of puzzle that is so big you can walk around. There is a very old one at Hampton Court. Herbert and I studied it in my "how to be a royal dog" lessons. The humans built them for fun. Normally there is a heart at the middle of every maze, so that you know you are halfway from the beginning and halfway to the end. The puzzle is to find your way out – and in some cases it can take a long time.'

Prince George had run back to the nursery and was jumping up and down whilst throwing his blanket and cushions at Sir Francis's ghost. 'LET'S

BUILD A MAZE!' he said happily.

The Duchess came into the nursery looking for her son. She didn't see the ghostly captain. George was not happy about having to leave the animals; he wanted to stay with them and have an adventure. 'Her Majesty would like to say hello to you. Come along, George, let's go and see her and then you can have some dinner.'

Holly and Lupo watched as the young boy held his mother's hand and followed her out of the room. Kitty waited until they had gone. She pulled off the blanket George had thrown over her head. 'So where is this maze?'

Holly went over to the library and found a book on Hampton Court. She flicked to the pages which showed a large maze, with a statue and a seating area at its centre. 'Somehow I don't think it's the maze at Hampton Court. If there was something there it would have been found by now. Besides, it's not a Tudor maze. It was built a long time after.'

Kitty heard something moving in the corner of the room. Running over to it she saw several palace mice in smart overalls. 'What's going on here?' she asked them.

'It's Herbert, ma'am. We have news,' said the tiny mouse agent.

'Please tell me. Is he all right?' Lupo asked.

Herbert was lost in thought as he clicked open the secret entrance to Mice Intelligence 5 HQ at the Peter Pan statue in Hyde Park. Wearily he made his way down to his office.

Once inside the peace and quiet of his messy workroom he poured himself a large cup of cold tea. Until he was sure of what he knew, he decided not to tell any of his mice agents about the maze or Sir Francis's ghost. Several hours had passed and it was only when Issy appeared with an iced bun that he finally took his muddy paws off of his desk and stood up with some authority.

'Here, a nice iced bun for you.' She put the pastry down on top of a stack of unread reports. 'Nice and sticky, just the way you like it.'

'Thank you Issy, I'm very hungry.' His paws reached out for the sumptuous treat and he stuffed half the bun into his cheeks. 'I found something under Kensington Gardens.'

Issy cleared a small leather armchair of papers

and books and sat down.

'Herbert, I hope you don't mind. I took the liberty of sending a team to Kensington Palace to let Lupo know that you were safely back. It seems he was rather concerned about your whereabouts.'

'He was concerned about me? But I am the Head of Mice Intelligence 5! Ah, he is such a good dog.'

Absentmindedly Herbert picked up the other half of the bun and began munching big mouthfuls of the delicious, sweet, sticky icing. He was terribly tired. It had been a very long day. Removing his mud-stained glasses, he wiped them clean and put them back on. Finally, he was able to see the terrible state of his office. He was very embarrassed.

'Oh um, gosh this place is in a bit of a state. I don't suppose we can blame Kitty for the mess this time?' He glanced at his piles of notes, opened reference books and well-chewed pencils. Even his shelf full of awards looked badly in need of a good dusting.

Issy watched as the Head of MI5 attempted to pick through the mess. 'No, this was all you,' she said. 'I could give you a hand clearing it up if you like? I'll bet if we clean up all this dust we'll find things that have been lost for a lifetime!' she joked. 'You were about to tell me about something that you'd found?'

Herbert leapt into the air, knocking the remainder of his bun on to Issy's lap. 'THAT'S IT!' He had his answer. 'Oh sorry . . . Hurry! There is little time to waste. Send a mapping team down to the City of Creatures. Beyond the river there is a . . . WAIT no . . . hang on . . . we can't, it might have all kinds of traps!'

Issy was utterly confused as she watched Herbert running around the room, raiding filing cabinets and rummaging through drawers. 'I have never seen you behave so erratically. Map what? Traps? What are you looking for now?'

'I'm looking for animal coins! We will need them to trade at the market!'

Issy was curious. 'Trade at the market? I don't understand.'

'I believe last night's storm uncovered a maze under Kensington Palace. Not just any maze!'

'A maze, under Kensington?' questioned Issy.

'The problem is, there are two large stone Minotaurs guarding the entrance – with big horns

68

and everything. Quite a sight, let me tell you.'
Herbert began throwing around books and papers.
'I think there is something living beyond the maze.
When I discovered it I noticed flickering lights.
When I asked if there was anyone there, no one
replied, but whatever is beyond that maze has been
there for some time, of that I am sure. And another
thing: that cave was so well covered up, it's the ideal
hiding place for . . .'

Issy jumped up. 'You think it's the hiding place of
the *Golden Hind*!'

Herbert grabbed at the pockets of his favourite
cardigan, checking to see what was in them. Then he
sped out of the door and ran towards the mouse
tunnel that would take him all the way to Kensington
Palace. 'EXACTLY, MY DEAR! FIND THAT
GHOST. SIR FRANCIS IS THE KEY TO
GETTING US SAFELY THROUGH THAT
MAZE! HURRY!' he shouted as he ran.

The Queen was happily playing with Prince George.
He was bouncing around on her lap. The Duke
was laughing at Princess Charlotte who was
pretending to bark at Vulcan.

Vulcan, meanwhile, was scowling at the happy family. He could see the weather had much improved and he couldn't work out why they had to stay for dinner.

Willow, the Queen's old Corgi, tried to cheer him up. 'It's a force nine gale outside. We shouldn't be going anywhere. No, it's best we stay here and have a nice dinner with the family.'

Candy was admiring the Duchess's footwear. 'Lovely shoes she has. If we are going to be here for a while I might go and take a peak in her closet. I'd love to see her ballgown collection.' Vulcan watched as the corgi Candy stealthily moved out of the room.

If only he could escape. Unfortunately, he was stuck here. Holly had gone off with Lupo and neither of them had been seen all afternoon. 'What are they up to?' he thought to himself.

'. . . and the house is just wonderful. We will be so happy there,' said the Duchess to the Queen. 'It is a shame to be leaving London. But we'll be back.'

Vulcan relished the future. Soon enough, Lupo would be gone to the countryside and at last he would have the run of the palaces to himself. The royal spaniel's time for adventures was coming to an end.

Herbert dived past Vulcan. Not a single human reacted. The mouse moved with such skill he completely avoided crashing into the butler who was serving a fresh pot of tea. Willow had also spotted the mouse. She watched as the Head of MI5 bounced on a cucumber sandwich and flew down the sofa towards the fireplace. 'He is so skilled!' she said with glee to a seething Vulcan.

Vulcan decided to follow the mouse. Something was going on and he wasn't about to be left out.

Herbert wriggled under the doorway to the Nursery and was delighted to see that Kitty, Holly and Lupo were all together. On the floor in front of them was the strange wooden dog that had fallen off the model and next to it stood a rather frightened and intimidated junior mouse.

Lupo was the first to speak while Herbert tried to catch his breath. 'Herbert, I'm glad to see you are OK! Your agent here took the trouble to explain that you have been on quite a journey.'

Kitty slunk around the plump brown mouse

in his smart green cardigan. 'Not cool, Herbie. So not cool. Lupo's been pacing. He nearly wore a hole in the carpet!'

'May I remind you Kitty, my name is Herbert. Not Herbie or "Scrummy Mouse" or "Tiny Dinner" for that matter.' Herbert pushed the tabby cat's sharp claws out of his way. 'Holly, as ever it's a delight to see you. Lupo, I apologise, it's taken me a while to figure it all out and get back to you. There is much to explain.'

The tiny mouse agent scuttled off, happy to put some distance between himself and the famous palace cat who was eyeing him up like something she wanted to devour for dinner.

Holly had been examining the wooden dog. She put it down so that she could greet Herbert properly. 'Hello, Herbert. I'm so glad you are all right. We were all very worried about you.' Herbert hugged Holly's paw.

'I'm quite well, but thank you for your concern.' He looked at the dog. 'Now, what's this?'

'It fell out of the model,' she said, pushing the paper scroll towards the clever mouse and pointing her nose up to the model ship, now back on the bookcase. 'And perhaps you would like to be introduced to him.' Herbert picked up the piece of paper and examined it.

'Introduced? To who?' Herbert said as he examined the rolled up paper.

Kitty looked confused. 'To the ghost in the corner of the room!'

Herbert slowly inched around. 'Sir Francis Drake, may I say it is an honour and a pleasure to make your acquaintance. I believe I have found the whereabouts of your ship.'

Vulcan sat behind the door to the nursery. He had heard enough. 'So the race is on to find the *Golden Hind*,' he mused. His thoughts flicked back to his meeting with Ebony at the Katz Bar.

He had confidently entered the establishment, sure that his plan to get all the information he needed out of her would be easy. The only thing that he hadn't prepared himself for was Ebony's gang. From the moment he entered, he felt eyes watching his every move. Vulcan carefully made himself as comfortable as possible in a corner booth. There were two cats near the bar squabbling over spilt milk.

Ebony was watching him from behind the bar. Her green eyes stared right through him as she gracefully walked towards his table. Two small cats rushed over, showering her with their adoration.

'GO!' she purred pointedly. 'Milk times two. Make his cold. Mine I'd like warm and make sure no one bothers us. Vulcan and I have much to discuss.'

Vulcan removed his hood and growled, 'I thought we'd agreed no names. It's not a good thing if people see me here. Did you bring the treasure map?'

Ebony spied Vulcan with suspicious eyes. 'Tell me everything you know, then I'll show you the map. My house, my rules.'

The milk was dumped on to the table in a pair of bowls and the two small cats kicked out the residents who had been merrily enjoying themselves, before a crocodile and a lizard locked the bar's doors. They stood guard so as not to let anyone in.

Vulcan didn't relish his chances against the crocodile. 'You have been busy. A bar full of thugs and there was Lupo thinking you would quietly slip into the background, never to been seen or heard from again. What a mistake he made . . .'

Ebony didn't move. 'I didn't want you to

come here to flatter me, Vulcan. I invited you here for answers.'

Vulcan was stuck. He wanted the treasure map. 'It's not just any treasure map. If I'm right, and I won't know for sure until I see that map, then it points the way to the *Golden Hind*.'

'The *Golden Hind*?' It was not a name Ebony was familiar with. She wanted Vulcan to give away as much information as he could before she let 'Chump' the crocodile and 'Lump' the lizard eat the royal dog for their dinner.

'Yes. It was one of Queen Elizabeth I's ships. It has been lost for hundreds of years. A lot of people thought that it had been destroyed. But apparently not. No, your map could lead to us solving one of the biggest mysteries of all time. You see, there was a lot of gold on board that ship when it disappeared.'

Ebony wasn't satisfied and needed more. 'Disappeared?'

Vulcan sneered; he was growing weary of her attitude. 'Look, Ebony, either you have a map or you don't. I have told you enough.' The black cat looked suspiciously at Vulcan. He ignored her stare.

Ebony didn't like Vulcan. He was a snivelling

no-good dog and if he was interested in this *Golden Hind* it was for a much bigger reason than he was letting on. 'Doesn't sound like much to me, this ship. What have you got to gain from finding it anyway?'

Vulcan shrugged. 'I like history.'

Ebony held up her paw, unhappy with the Queen's dorgi's answer. Chump the crocodile slid forwards. She pointed at Vulcan and said, 'EAT HIM!'

Quick as a flash, the crocodile was next to Vulcan. In two moves it had Vulcan's cape in its thick jaws. Vulcan was quite scared. 'ALL RIGHT, all right, I'll tell you. Just get rid of your pet.'

Ebony hissed and Chump backed off.

Vulcan decided that now was not the time for holding back. A little bit of history might even help him to convince her to show him the map. 'The *Golden Hind* ran into a Spanish ship filled to bursting with treasure. There was a battle and the *Golden Hind* won. There was enough treasure on board to fill England's empty treasury,' he explained. 'There was a huge party when the ship came into port. The whole of England celebrated. The only thing was that as the fireworks popped, the ship went missing. All that is left are clues as to where it might be. I found one of them in a book in the library at Buckingham Palace. The book told me that there was a map that would guide you to the secret entrance to the ship's hiding place. I believe you have that map.'

Ebony was smiling. She liked the idea of being needed. 'I would be happy with a big ship of my own. But, Vulcan, I have seen into your dark soul and I know you want much, much more. What do you plan on doing once you find the *Golden Hind*?'

For the first time that day, Vulcan smiled. 'Gold buys you power and power is all I want.'

Ebony lifted the bowl to her whiskers. 'And if I take you to the secret entrance to the ship? What then?'

'Are you prepared to share your throne with me?' Vulcan questioned her readiness to give away so much. After all, she was the one who had found the map.

It was Ebony's turn to smile. 'The map isn't here, but I will bring it to you. In my experience, Vulcan, every dog has its day and yours is well overdue. Here's to us. Here's to power!'

* * *

Herbert finished telling them all about the maze he had found. 'So you see, all we have to do is make our way through the maze and then *ta-da!* We have found the *Golden Hind*!' The ghost was impressed. 'And your missing dog, of course, Sir Francis.'

Holly was concerned. 'Herbert, it's a maze. It might be very hard to find our way around it. Are you sure it's a good idea that we go?'

'We can all be pirates!' said Lupo. He loved ships, the sea and a good mystery. He often played pirates with George. The little prince would dress up in his costume with his stripy shirt and cut-off trousers, even putting an eye-patch over his eye. Nanny was great at painting skulls and crossbones on to the prince's pink cheeks. Best of all, they would both wear matching bandanas.

Holly could see how excited Lupo was. The royal spaniel was panting! She laughed. 'Lupo, I never knew you liked pirates so much!'

To prove to her just how much he liked dressing up he ran over to the dressing up box and pulled out his bandana. Carefully, he tied it around Kitty's head and then he took out George's bandana and tied it around his neck. Kitty shook her head. 'Get this silly thing off me!'

'This is great. Let's go! Now we look the part!' he said happily.

Herbert was less enthusiastic. 'Lupo, perhaps Holly is right. Those two Minotaurs meant business. They were a warning of danger.'

Kitty blew a raspberry, breaking the sober mood in the room. 'Danger? Ships full of gold? Lupo, when was your last flea treatment?'

Lupo cocked his head to one side. Herbert sat back down. Lupo put his paw on top of the wooden dog. 'Please, everyone. This might be the last big adventure we have for some time. I move to the country next week and I just want to have one last big adventure. A fun one. Please?'

Sir Francis walked over to the window. 'I'm sorry I can't go myself. But I can help you all if you decide to go. I can give you instructions on how to get through the maze.' The ghost shrugged and then sat down on the corner of the little blue sofa awaiting the animals' decision.

Kitty pulled the bandana off her head. 'Look, everyone, I'll miss you when you are not around and I have to say I really love our time together. It's just that this sounds like it could be muddy and I'm just not into that. Besides, "Small Supper" won't want me tagging along.'

Everyone laughed together until Herbert put his paws on his hips. 'SMALL SUPPER? That's a new one. Kitty, I don't think it's possible for us to have an adventure without you. I say we *all* go. Lupo's right: this could be the last adventure we have for a while. Come on, Kitty. I'd really like it if you'd come with us.'

8

The Adventure Begins

Kitty had reluctantly agreed to come and was wearing Prince George's pirate scarf. Herbert was clutching a similar scarf that had pink polka dots, which Princess Charlotte had insisted that he take with him. Lupo had his bandana on, of course.

'It looks like everyone's ready,' Holly said.

Herbert held the scarf up. 'We just need to stop off in the City of Creatures and pick up a few supplies. We can put everything in here. A most handy invention, the bandana.'

The grandfather clock in the hallway chimed loudly, and it was time to leave.

As the group of animals walked into the pantry, Lupo said, 'Hey, I know a pirate song. Anyone want to hear it?'

There once was a ship, sailing on the sea, sailing on
*   the sea, sailing on the sea,*
The ship was filled to bursting with gold, filled with
*   gold and treasure you see,*
One day a pirate just like me – swung on board and
*   swiped all the gold!*
With a swish and swoosh my sword went slosh and
*   I was a pirate dog,*
Sailing on the sea!

They all laughed at Lupo's song. Meanwhile, Vulcan
followed closely behind them in the shadows – not
daring to lose them for a second.

The storm had delayed Ebony's expedition with
Vulcan to the *Golden Hind*. She flicked coins into a
jar on the bar and watched as her army tussled and
bickered with each other, eager for something to do.
The map was laid out in front of her. A coin landed
on the corner of it and as she swished the coin away
she sat up. The map was a detailed drawing of
corridors and tunnels that all led to a large 'X'. Exactly
where the coin had landed, Ebony noticed what
looked like the initials 'KP'. She rubbed the bottom

of her chin and her long whiskers tickled.

'WHERE ARE MY MICE? FIND THEM AND BRING THEM HERE NOW!' she commanded.

Three blind wise mice ran as fast as they could across the bar and crashed into the bottom of the stool she was sitting on.

'There you are. On the map there are the initials "KP". They seem to be written directly under a large building. Tell me, is there a secret passage under Kensington Palace?'

The mice were shocked. No one but the royal pets knew about the Red route. None of them spoke up. They decided to stay very quiet, but Ebony was smart. 'I can tell by your silence that there is something you are not telling me. TELL ME NOW OR I WILL EAT EVERY ONE OF YOU!'

The three wise mice were far too frightened to stay quiet. They squeaked together, 'Yes. There is a secret passage. It's the Red route.'

Ebony ran her scratchy tongue over her paw with satisfaction. 'The Red route, how very interesting. Now, who needs Vulcan? We have everything we need. Come on, we're leaving,' she said, grabbing the map off the bar.

The three mice scuttled away, happy not to have been eaten. Chump the crocodile stood looking at the map over Ebony's shoulder. 'It's a long walk through those tunnels and then it looks like we will have to swim.' Chump was happy: it had been ages since he had been in the water and his scales felt dry and itchy.

Ebony snatched the map away from Chump's prying eyes. She hated having to have the crocodile and lizard in her crew. He was right, though, and thankfully there were enough animals to carry her across the water. As they all made their way out of the bar she just hoped that they wouldn't come across any more of the Crocodile King's beasts on their travels.

The Crocodile King loved his treasure. He ate from golden plates and slept in a bed made of thousands of coins. He even strutted around his 'hive' of filthy beasts wearing a crown he had fashioned from bits of jewellery and precious gems the humans had thrown into the River Thames. The monsters he lived with called him the King of the Thames and they scuttled around him, obeying his every order.

Once her scruffy gang of cats found out about the map, it was only a matter of time before she got a message that the Crocodile King wanted to meet with her. Ebony had been summoned and no one disobeyed such an invitation.

The King squirmed with joy at the thought of getting his slimy croc claws on his share of the gold. Ebony narrowly avoided being eaten by promising to deliver at least half of whatever she found on the ship. He offered her a trade: Chump and Lump would help as long as she returned the minute she had the gold.

She looked at Chump and Lump. They were ready to collect their master's treasure. If she didn't return with the treasure, she would have to face the King and the prospect of being eaten herself. She had to succeed, her very existence depended on it.

Sir Francis had warned them that he had waited almost a hundred years for a storm big enough to uncover the maze under Kensington Palace. He had said that they had until the storm had passed to work their way through the maze. Herbert had taken notes, scribbling frantically into his notebook. The ghost explained, 'You have little time, so use it wisely.'

Lupo was carrying Herbert on his back and Kitty was running alongside him. Holly was doing her best to keep up, but it was hard with such short legs. 'I don't understand why we are running. It's an old ship! It's not as if it is going anywhere!' she said.

'Well, that's not exactly true,' replied Herbert in a shaky voice. 'Sir Francis was right. Once the storm has passed, we will have to deal with all the extra floodwater. Things are pretty bad down in the city already. If the waters get any higher the maze could be lost at any moment.'

Everyone stopped along the plush royal Red route. One by one they looked at each other, horrified.

Holly was the first to speak. 'Hang on a moment. Are you saying that we could be heading into a maze that could just disappear?'

Herbert nodded emphatically. 'Quite literally, yes.' The mouse patted the outside of his cardigan, looking for his notebook. When he finally found it, he hastily thumbed past pages of directions he had taken from Sir Francis. 'The maze has been lost under water for over 400 years. The only reason it hasn't completely crumbled to nothing is because it is sheltered in a rather interesting cave system, which for all intents and purposes is supporting the entire structure.'

Kitty rolled her eyes. 'Told you this was a bad idea. No one ever listens to the cat.'

'According to Sir Francis, we will face our first challenge at the entrance to the maze. It could be quite dangerous,' Herbert said. 'We will have to face the Minotaur statues. The book says that it will not be easy. One mistake and we could all lose our heads.'

Holly felt queasy. 'You said that the Minotaurs will be our first challenge, so what are the others?' She was thinking about the journey ahead of them. 'How many are there?'

Herbert studied his notebook. 'Oh dear, Sir Francis didn't exactly say how many challenges we might face.' As they ran down the Red route, Herbert tried to calm everyone's nerves. 'It might be like the maze at Hampton Court. You know, it's really quite

 pleasant: green trees everywhere and it even has an ice cream stand at the end of it.'

88

Lupo smiled. 'Herbert, by the look of your face I'd say that even you don't think we are going to find an ice cream stand in our maze.'

Sir Francis's directions led them down to the heart of the City of Creatures. By the time they arrived, all of them were out of breath apart from Herbert who was making a list of things they would need. Sir Francis had said that they could expect the unexpected and Herbert wanted to make sure they were all well prepared.

The bustling night market was in full swing with all kinds of creatures selling things from rows and rows of stalls. Lupo was amazed to see a cat selling blackbird pies on one stall and right next to it there was a chicken surrounded by fresh eggs screeching, 'Adopt a chick today.' He passed a fox and a magpie who had gathered quite a crowd around their stall: they had been busy collecting all kinds of things from the humans up top. Lupo could see that they were doing a roaring trade in boats they had fashioned out of plastic shopping bags. The fox was shouting, 'These boats will float like a dream on the floodwaters! Trade your goods for one today!'

ADOPT A CHICKEN TODAY

BLACKBIRD PIE

'Perhaps we ought to see what they are selling: those boats might come in handy. Shall we have a look, Herbert?' asked Lupo.

Herbert yanked Lupo and Holly to one side. 'First, down here it's a bit different. If they recognise you, we will have a lot of animals asking what we are up to and I don't think we need that kind of attention. After all, the maze could be tricky enough without having anyone following us. So be careful. You will need to trade for items using these.' He reached into his pocket and pulled out a small bag of coins. 'Animal coins. Now, here's the list,' he said, handing Holly a torn-out page from his little pocket notebook. 'You two hurry along; remember we don't have long and those floodwaters are rising.' Herbert then turned his attention to Kitty. 'You and I are going to pay a visit to the Katz Bar. I want to see what our old friend Ebony is up to. And Lupo, one more thing – no, those boats are nothing more than plastic bags – they will sink not float!'

Holly read the list aloud.

LIST OF THINGS REQUIRED FOR OUR ADVENTURE

3x Buttons

1x Hairclip

1x Can of fizzy drink (just in case anyone gets thirsty)

3x Bags of Catnip (just in case anyone needs to distract some nasty alley cats)

1x Box of Matches

4x Candles

1x Small Pocket Mirror

When she was finished, she looked back at Herbert. 'This is a very strange list of objects. I'm not sure I understand what they are for.'

Herbert smiled. 'Never mind the drink or the catnip – those we can do without – but the other things on that list – trust me, those are exactly the objects we need. I want us to be prepared for anything in that maze.'

Vulcan has been following the four friends closely. He briefly watched as they shopped in the night market. From his hiding place behind a stall, he could see the Katz Bar selling slimy sewer fish. Ebony and her crew were moving out, the map gripped tightly in her sharp claws. He growled, 'She's going to find the treasure – she's not waiting for me. I *knew* I couldn't trust that cat!'

Vulcan was uneasy. He had to quickly decide who to follow: Ebony with the map or Lupo and his friends. In the end, Chump the crocodile helped make the decision easier. Vulcan watched as he snapped his jaws at some visiting kittens. He felt it would be better to stick with the palace creatures then be caught following Ebony and her dangerous river animals.

Vulcan's dark eyes watched as Ebony slunk into the darkness of an old sewer tunnel. Then he turned back to watch the Palace Four. He could hear them agreeing to meet at the Katz Bar in an hour. There they would double-check that they had everything needed for their journey around the maze. Vulcan whispered to himself: 'Clever little mouse! That's right – you do all the work. Find me the golden ship before Ebony does!'

Lupo and Holly began looking for the things on Herbert's list. It was easy for them both to get distracted. There was so much to see in the bustling night market.

There were all kinds of animals, large and small, mingling and trading. Thankfully, they all seemed too busy to notice the royal dogs as they walked around, studying the stalls and occasionally stopping to examine things more closely.

Holly found a pretty pink hairclip, which looked like it had once belonged to a little girl. She picked it up and showed Lupo. 'Here, look! Do you think this is what Herbert had in mind? I can't imagine what it's good for in a maze!' She opened and closed the pretty clip.

Lupo nodded. 'Yes, I think it's probably exactly what he was wanting. Though I do agree, it all seems a bit odd.'

Politely Holly asked the stall seller, a fat buck rat, 'Please sir, how much for the hairclip?' Then, spotting a small pocket mirror, she picked it up and said, 'This too? How much for both?'

The buck rat eyed both dogs. He knew exactly who they were. The last time he had seen Holly and Lupo they were at the Tower of London causing mischief for him and his master, Edgar the raven. Now the royal dogs were in the City of Creatures. Edgar would want to know why. Claw eyed the two with greedy, hungry eyes. 'Good evening to you both,' he said creepily. 'How fascinating, a pair of royal dogs, trading in the marketplace, at night!'

Lupo growled.

The rat wasn't about to end his questions. Ever since the royal dogs turned the Tower of London upside down, discovered the secret of Windsor Castle and set Ebony the ancient Egyptian cat loose amongst the sewers, all the royal dogs had been carefully watched by Edgar. The raven wasn't about to let Lupo and his friends cause any more trouble. Claw had only recently recovered from having to spend far too much time with the Crocodile King, under the river, clearing up Lupo's last adventure.

'Curious . . . you want to trade for a hairclip and a mirror. What are you two looking for?'

Lupo had a bad feeling about the rat. He also had the strangest sense that their paths had crossed before.

Holly grabbed the clip and mirror and quickly stuck the clip in her fur, using the mirror to adjust it. 'You see, it just looks so pretty on me, I just have to have them both! You never know when a mirror will come in handy!'

Claw looked at her suspiciously.

Lupo snatched back the buck rat's gaze. 'Never you mind. What's the price for the things? Or, if you would prefer, we can go somewhere else.'

'Two coins. I'll give you them both for one if you tell me why you're down here?' Claw suggested.

Holly looked nervously at Lupo, but he stood firm. 'Two it is.'

He handed two animal coins to the buck rat who bowed ever so slightly as he tucked the coins into his pouch. 'Good evening and thank you . . . your Royal Highnesses.'

Lupo felt a great sense of unease. The familiar rat had rattled his nerves. 'At least we have two of the items on the list, now all we need are the buttons and . . .'

Holly pointed to a stall on the far side of the market. 'Matches and candles! Look over there!' She was looking at a smart-looking barn owl. 'He's got what we need. Come on. Let's get as far away from that rat at possible!'

The owl was very pleased to have not one but two royal dogs trading at his stall. 'It is a very great honour to meet you both. Lupo, I have heard so much about you! Tales of your adventures have spread far and wide. Please, please, how can I help you. *Twit-twoooo!*'

They managed to get the other items before Holly and Lupo felt water under their paws. Lupo could see that the entire market was starting to flood. 'We'd better find Herbert and get out of here.'

Vulcan looked away. He couldn't watch Lupo looking tenderly at Holly. 'Holly doesn't need you because she has me,' he muttered. A beetle ran beneath him, and, as if to demonstrate his anger, he cruelly drowned it under his paw. 'I will crush you, Lupo, like this beetle – enjoy this – for this is your very last adventure with my Holly!'

9
Three Blind Mice

Herbert and Kitty were inside the Katz Bar. It was strangely quiet. Kitty felt uncertain. 'I don't think I have ever seen it so empty. Mind you, it's probably because, these days, this place is run by Ebony. That cat gives me the chills. Talk about nine lives – Ebony must be on at least her twelfth by my count.'

The Head of MI5 wasn't listening to Kitty. The ends of his whiskers were picking up a very familiar vibration from the floor. All of a sudden, he was up and off.

Kitty watched the soft brown mouse in his green cardigan running into a small opening on the corner of the bar. 'WHERE ARE YOU GOING NOW?' she shouted after him.

Herbert replied in a loud whisper, 'The bar is too clean!'

He was right. Kitty remembered the bar being very different before Ebony took it over. In the past it had been covered in cat hair and discarded milk bottles. It wasn't only the cleanliness of the place that seemed unusual: bits of once broken furniture now seemed to have been carefully repaired. 'PALACE MICE!' she whispered under her breath. 'Where are they hiding, Herbert?'

Herbert climbed into the corner of the bar. He was unsurprised to find three blind mice inside. 'What's going on in here?' Herbert asked the scraggily mice.

'I KNEW HE'D COME!' said one of the mice.

'HE'S LOOKING FOR THE LOST PIRATE,' mumbled another.

'We can't see you, but we can smell you,' said the last mouse. 'Come on, let's give him to Ebony. Bet she'd be interested in what the Head of MI5 is doing snooping around the Katz Bar.'

'You three can start by telling me just what you are doing down here. I can spot a palace mouse's handiwork anytime. And don't tell me you're down here because it's better paid!'

The three blind mice leaned in to talk to one another and then answered together. 'IT IS BETTER PAID!'

Lupo and Holly found Kitty with her backside in the air, and her eyes trained on a spot in the corner of the room.

She turned round to see them. 'Quick, you two, Herbert's down there with three palace mice. They just said something about a "lost pirate" and it sounds like they work for Ebony. It's all a bit odd if you ask me. Herbert is trying to talk to them.'

Holly looked around the bar cautiously. 'If this is supposed to be Ebony's bar, then where is she?'

Lupo spotted a jar of coins on the bar top. 'Ebony's gone. And she left in a bit of a hurry. Didn't even bother to put her hard-earned coins away,' he said, tapping the jar.

Herbert emerged from the hole with the mice. Kitty stood over them ready to pounce.

All three blind mice sniffed the air, and one of them spoke up. 'We can't see him but we can tell – he is here amongst us. The One. The gatekeeper.'

Lupo looked at his friends. 'Herbert, we should

be getting on. What do these mice know that we don't?'

'Oh, he's young and foolish. That is good.'

'Young and foolish.'

'Foolish and young. Very good.' The three mice said to each other.

Kitty had heard enough. 'I'm going to eat them.'

'Wait,' said Herbert, leaping in Kitty's way. 'These aren't ordinary mice. They were pushed out of the palace a few years ago. They scared all the younger mice with their strange stories.'

The three mice nodded. 'We tried to warn them all. No one would listen. Then Ebony came along. She offered us a warm home, somewhere we could take care of her. In return we shared all our knowledge.'

Herbert looked concerned. 'What did you tell her about this lost pirate?'

The three mice once again huddled together. 'Nothing. She knows nothing of the pirate.'

Lupo spoke up. 'The lost pirate?'

The three mice gathered around Lupo. 'The lost pirate got left behind; legend says that she guards the treasure and that she is a savage beast. She sails the ship with no crew. All alone, a ghost in every way, but living to this day!' The three mice then all said together, 'Whisper!'

'Sir Francis's missing dog!' said Lupo.

Kitty loomed over the mice. 'Where is Ebony now?'

The mice cowered behind Herbert. 'She's gone with the others to find the ship. She has a map!'

Herbert spoke first. 'Oh dear, not only will we have to deal with the floodwaters, but we may very well run into Ebony and her vicious thugs.'

Holly was not about to be defeated. 'Lupo and I got everything on your list, Herbert. I suggest we get going before it's too late. Who knows what kind of terror Ebony could cause with all that treasure. We now have even more of a reason to find the *Golden Hind*. We must stop her.'

The three blind mice could feel the friends getting ready to leave. Lupo felt sorry for the funny-looking mice. He leant in to thank them. 'I'm sorry you felt that you had to leave the palace. You could return if you wanted to. I'd be happy to make you welcome at Kensington. Bernie, the Head Mousekeeper, could do with some wise new friends.'

The mice liked Lupo. 'You are a fine dog, Lupo.' Then they spoke softly into his ear so that the others could not hear them. 'You are the gatekeeper, Lupo. You'll find a way through the great maze. Use all your senses! Beware of an evil dog because he will be hot on your tail.'

They all left the Katz Bar feeling very uneasy.

The night market was closed and only a few creatures were left clearing up. Lupo chose to listen to the mice's warning. He kept looking around to check that they weren't being followed. If there was someone watching them, then he was doing a very good job keeping well hidden.

Holly was yawning by the time they reached the edge of the city. They were all standing at the entrance to a narrow sewer tunnel. Rats and insects crawled along the tunnel walls, looking for shelter from the high floodwaters. It was a dark and damp place. 'Where are we?' she asked fearfully.

Kitty didn't like how close they were to the rising water. Nervously, she spoke. 'Herbert, are you quite sure that taking this route is a good idea? You and I both know what it's like. What if we run into trouble?'

Herbert pointed to two large planks of wood tied up alongside a makeshift pier on the side of the tunnel. They floated on top of the fast-moving water. 'We will need to use those to go the rest of the way.'

The colour drained from Kitty's face. Water. And worse: moving water. All her fears were realised when she saw the sunken plastic shopping bags floating by with unhappy animals cursing the fox who had tricked them into believing they would make good boats.

'I AM NOT GETTING ON TO THAT RAFT THING!' Kitty added. 'DON'T MAKE ME! I DON'T WANT TO.' Herbert ignored the palace cat's pleading. 'There has to be another way round,' she said. 'Tell you what, everyone, I will go and look for it. You guys carry on.'

'Kitty, there is no other way around,' answered Herbert. 'Now Holly, you make sure you hang on tight. Lupo can swim, so if we get into any kind of trouble, he can help you and Kitty. Make sure you don't fall in, and that means you too, Kitty. The sewers are no place for royal pets.' Holly saw the plank and looked unhappily over to Lupo.

Lupo patted her paw gently. 'It's OK, I will be right behind you.'

Kitty rolled her eyes 'ER . . . UM . . . I AM NOT HAPPY! Is anyone paying attention? LOOK, in case you lot have forgotten. I am a cat. I don't swim anywhere.'

Holly patted Kitty on the back. 'You heard, Herbert: it's the only way to the maze. We have to get going, and I promise to take care of you. You won't fall in. OK?'

Herbert watched as Kitty and Holly carefully walked on to the floats and began paddling downstream, using their paws. 'Lupo and I will be right behind you. I marked the way in. We will need to travel downstream until we see the sign I left. Keep an eye out for it.'

Vulcan pushed aside a small family of mice who were begging at his feet for a lift, almost treading on one tiny creature who couldn't be more than a few days old. 'OUT OF MY WAY!' he scolded.

Somehow, he would have to stop Edgar and Claw from disrupting his plans. He watched as Claw hurriedly packed up his stall. It would only be a matter of time before the raven found out that the royal animals were in the city. Vulcan hadn't counted on having to deal with Edgar.

Vulcan has left the three blind mice more than a little shaken up. He was annoyed that Ebony had gone ahead. Thanks to those silly mice, Lupo and his friends had been able to walk into the bar and get their information, then walk out without anyone attempting to stop them. The race to find the *Golden Hind* was on and Vulcan was prepared to do whatever it took to get to the fabled gold before Ebony. Even if meant going for a swim in the sewer.

10
A Wondrous Fear

The floodwaters in the sewers were even higher than Herbert remembered. Hundreds of black rats had built temporary homes along the banks. The school run for the rats was normally a quick swim, then a hop on to the bankside and a dash into the schoolhouse. Since the schoolhouse had been washed away along with everything else, the new structure was being built to last, with plastic bottles and a few old car tyres. Better still, the young animals had been given plastic bottle boats on a pulley system to travel up and down the high floodwaters.

Mrs Claw was delighted with the new arrangement. Better still, Claw was in good spirits: he had dashed off early to the Tower of London to speak to his master, Edgar the raven. She had finished cheerfully waving off all 120 of her younglings before getting on with the job of cleaning and maintaining their new nest.

She had just finished making the younglings' beds when she saw Holly and Kitty floating past her home, followed by Lupo and Herbert. She leant out of the window to see if she could see where they were going. That was when she spotted Vulcan. He was under several newspapers – half in the water and half out. She'd remembered his face from the last time he'd come to visit them. He'd been awfully rude and quite frightening.

'That terrible Vulcan. He's following them. Claw will have something to say about all this. I won't have that awful dorgi down in my sewer.' She bustled out of her home and headed in the direction of the Tower of London. 'We'll see what Edgar has to say about this!'

Lupo was only just managing to hang on to the plank. He could see that, ahead, Holly and Kitty were struggling to keep the plank flat on the fast moving water. Every now and then they would all have to re-balance to avoid being knocked off by tree trunks, upturned shopping trolleys and several beaten-up bicycles. The sewer was full of debris from the storm.

'Kitty, hang on! There is something coming up. Lean to the left a bit—' said Holly, trying to steer their plank.

'I want to get off this thing. I can't stand it!' Kitty called out. 'Lupo, are we nearly there yet?'

Herbert shook his head. 'I can't seem to see the mark. I know it's somewhere around here!'

Lupo looked around the walls and the ceiling of the brick sewage tunnel. 'What does the mark look like?'

Herbert bounced on the raft, causing it to rock. 'THERE! I SEE IT!' he cried out. 'OVER THERE!'

Lupo steadied their float and looked for the mark. Finally, he spotted something. Above an entrance to a side tunnel was a rough drawing of two flowers. 'Herbert, is that it? There they are – two roses.'

'Well done, Lupo!' Herbert sounded gleeful.

Lupo barked back to the others, 'Holly, Kitty. It is. The roses! You'll need to steer yourselves towards that tunnel. All right?'

'I see it!' said Holly. 'Hang on, Kitty.'

From behind, Lupo watched as Holly skilfully

manoeuvered the float into line with the tunnel. Then the worst thing possible happened. Kitty slid right off the float and into the water. Holly also ended up falling in. Since neither corgi nor cat could swim, it was left to Lupo to try and rescue them both. Herbert had no choice but to follow them all.

Together, they pushed through the muddy, dirty water. Lupo felt something pulling on his neck. Turning around, he saw that Kitty was now hanging on to him for dear life. 'GET ME OUT OF HERE!' she screeched. 'I'm a palace cat . . . argggghhhhh.'

Holly was fighting to keep herself above the water. 'Lupo it's moving too fast,' she said as her pretty face dipped below the water and back up again. 'The water is pulling me away!'

'Kick hard! Head for the tunnel. It's over there!' He was swimming as fast as he could with Kitty on his back.

Herbert was a highly capable swimmer. Being small, he was able to get to the side tunnel first. Pulling at a slim branch sticking out of the brickwork, he stuck it into the water and tried his best to wedge it between a bicycle wheel and a large stone. 'HERE. Grab this!' he cried.

Vulcan pushed his raft into the side of the wall. He could see the problems the others were having up ahead. 'Come on, hurry up!' he groaned, barely able to hang on. The strong current beneath him was forcing him free. Any minute and they would see him. He too now had to kick hard against the fast water.

Holly barely made it to the branch. She then heaved herself out of the water and into the side tunnel. 'Quick, Herbert, see if you can catch them.'

Herbert bravely ran along the slim branch and wrapped his long tail around it to secure himself. 'You're nearly here. Lupo, catch me!' he shouted. 'You are only going to get one chance. If you overshoot, then you'll end up too far upstream to get back!'

Lupo could see Herbert reaching out. Catching his tiny paws wasn't going to be easy. As they came closer to the branch, he kicked hard with his back legs. 'Hey watch it, I'm trying to hang on back here,' cried Kitty.

'ONE, TWO, THREE!' Herbert yelled out.

Lupo forced his way through the water and Herbert just about managed to grab on to his collar.

'Kitty, use the branch to pull yourself up,' Lupo

said in a strained voice.

Kitty was too scared. 'I can't.'

Lupo couldn't hold on for much longer. 'Kitty, you have to. If you don't, we will both drift off.'

Herbert's little face was going red. He was hanging on to Lupo's collar with everything that he had. 'KITTY, YOU CAN DO IT!'

Bravely Kitty began to let go. A large stick floating by caught her back legs and she used it to clamber on to the branch. Holly reached down and helped, pulling the palace tabby into the tunnel. Lupo went next. Something sharp stabbed him under the water and he could feel real pain. He cried out, 'OUCH!' before heaving his wet, exhausted body into the narrow tunnel.

Herbert clambered in last and saw that the floor of the tunnel was covered in blood. Lupo had injured his leg very badly. 'That's not good. Kitty, untie the bandana from around his neck – we can use it to stop the bleeding,' Herbert ordered. 'Quickly!'

Holly assisted Herbert in tying up the bad leg. Lupo winced in agony. Holly looked very concerned. 'We have to go back. He can't carry on with that leg.'

Lupo managed to stand up. As long as he had the

use of three legs, he would be fine. 'It's just a scratch. I'm not going back. We have come too far now. Come on. Let's get going.'

The tunnel was covered in brown tiles and red bricks. It went on for what seemed like miles. Herbert reached into the polka dot bandana and lit one of the candles so at least they could find their way. 'We need to go quite a bit further. The good news is that there shouldn't be any more swimming. It looks much clearer: the flood waters seem to have passed.'

Holly shook the last of the water out of her coat. 'How's the leg, are you OK?'

Lupo was doing his best to walk on all of his paws. 'All good,' he replied, wincing through the pain.

They came to a fork in the dark tunnel. Herbert stopped. He thought he could hear someone coming down the tunnel behind him. Nothing stirred. So he carried on walking. 'It's this way.'

At that moment, Ebony was riding on the back of Chump the crocodile, travelling along a tunnel high above Herbert. Chump swerved left and Ebony nearly fell into the muddy sewer waters.

'CAREFUL!' she screeched. 'If I end up getting so

much as one single hair wet I'll make sure you end up in someone's pot for dinner!' The rest of her crew struggled along behind her. Lump looked back at the scared and bewildered cats. 'The palace is up ahead,' shouted Ebony. 'Everyone look out for brickwork.'

According to the map they were getting closer. She only needed to get them through three more tunnels, which hopefully wouldn't be blocked by the storm debris. That should bring them to the entrance to the Red route. She couldn't wait to get to the golden ship. The prospect of all that Spanish gold warmed her cold heart. 'SWIM FASTER, CHUMP! I want my gold!'

Kitty was trying not to moan, but all she wanted was to get somewhere dry. She hadn't got the warm milk at the Katz Bar, thanks to Ebony disappearing, and she had nearly drowned. This was not a good adventure. She was at the point of stopping and walking back when at last they reached the end of the tunnel.

Holly touched Kitty's paw and said, 'Have you ever seen anything so incredible?'

Kitty looked upwards. In the pale light from the

flickering candle she could see twinkling. Gold ran in veins along the walls. It was breathtaking.

'Herbert, where are we?' asked Lupo, as he reached out to touch the rocks around them.

The little mouse's face was beaming with joy in the soft light. 'We are nearly at the entrance to the maze. Hurry.'

Everyone stared at the sight ahead. Two enormous stone Minotaurs stood with their horns locked together, guarding a stone entrance.

'This is it,' Herbert said. 'Is everyone ready to go in?'

Nervously Holly took a step closer to the large sculptures. 'They look so real!'

She was about to cross over the line between the two beasts when Herbert ran to pull her back. 'Let me take a closer look first. Rest awhile, everyone. Sir Francis gave me some instructions on how to get past them safely.'

Lupo sat on the soft muddy ground. Looking around, he could see that they were in a large cave. There was a low light coming from somewhere in the distance. 'Is that you, Whisper?' he said softly, resting his sore leg. He decided it might be wise to save the candle in case they needed it later on so he blew it out, much to Kitty's annoyance.

'I was using that to keep warm! If you don't mind!' she blurted out.

Lupo tried his best not to laugh. The tabby's coat was covered in mud and the warmth of the candle had made her fur stick out in muddy patches. He'd never seen her looking so messy.

'Come and have a look at this. It's truly amazing!' said Herbert.

He was standing next to the foot of one of the Minotaurs. 'Look close, but whatever you do, don't cross over.'

Holly and Lupo leaned in for a better look. Herbert began to blow on the soft soil running between the two stone beasts, revealing a thin string. 'It's booby trapped!' said Herbert.

Kitty lay on the floor. 'That's it. I'm done. This entirely crazy adventure is doomed. Lupo was all "it'll be fun" and "surprise, surprise, we are about to cross into a danger zone". If you think that I am going to get my head chopped off by one of those statues, you are wrong! Wait, Lupo . . . where are you going?'

Lupo was sniffing the thread. He discovered a second line of string buried under the first one. 'Watch this, Kitty.' He found the pink hair clip inside the bandana. Very carefully, he attached the two strings to each other. 'I believe that should do it. Herbert, what do you think?'

'You've read my mind. Well done, Lupo!' Herbert picked up a nearby stone. 'Let's test it to see if the hairclip has done the job.' He threw the stone into the middle of the entrance and waited. Nothing happened. 'I think we can go in now.'

As she watched all her friends walk into the mouth of the maze, Kitty shuddered. Fear had crept in and she could feel her courage slipping away. 'I can do this!' She was trying to convince herself that all would be well.

One paw at a time, she edged her way over the hairclip. She was halfway across when she decided that they might need the hairclip so she turned around and unclipped it. Her back leg was almost across when all of a sudden the great big statues appeared to come to life.

Lupo turned around, horrified to see the statues blowing out clouds of dust from their noses and thrashing around on the ground, their horns searching for a victim. 'Kitty, RUN!'

Kitty tripped on the strings and fell flat on her face, a hoof of one of the Minotaurs *smack* between her face and her paw.

'GET ME OUT OF HERE!' she screamed.

Lupo ran to try and help her. The two angry sleeping giants looked very unhappy about being disturbed. Dust and stone fell everywhere as they swung heavily around and around, stomping their feet and snorting loudly.

Vulcan decided that this was the moment for him to cross over the strings himself and run into the maze and hide. There was so much dust from the statues that he slipped past them all without being seen and hid and waited for the beasts to finish Kitty off.

The dust settled and Vulcan was disappointed to see Herbert and Holly pulling Kitty away from the beasts before they unleashed their next weapon of destruction, determined to stop the visitors from entering the maze.

A fireball the size of a football flew at Lupo. The clever royal dog sprinted to safety. He pushed his friends out of the way of a second fireball and then it was over. The heavy stone heads of the Minotaur statues turned back to face each other. And in one moment, all hope of getting out was gone. The entrance to the maze was now closed. There was no way back. They had no choice but to brave the mysteries of the maze ahead.

11
Scary Snap!

Edgar hated surprises. Finding out that Lupo and his friends were in the City of Creatures would not normally be a cause for concern. But Claw had also told him that he'd seen the evil Vulcan in the shadows of the city, and Edgar's thin black feathers prickled uncomfortably. A sure sign something was going on. It is the job of the ravens at the Tower of London to protect England at all costs, and, in Edgar's opinion, especially from the likes of Vulcan. Edgar knew that Vulcan wanted the throne. He knew that Vulcan would stop at nothing to get all that he desired.

'We need to find out what Vulcan is up to, Claw.' He hopped around his small cell at the Tower. Claw's market stall had proved to be an unexpected source of information. 'We know, thanks to your stall, that

Vulcan is skulking around in the darkness. I think Lupo, Holly, Herbert and Kitty are all looking for the *Golden Hind*.'

Mrs Claw burst into his cell with news of a daring swim along one of the most unpleasant sewers in London – adding to Edgar's suspicions that a royal pet quest was afoot.

Edgar rubbed his beak against the soft stone. 'And what of the Crocodile King, Claw? He's been rather quiet of late. His huge nest beneath the Thames is now completed and I have it on good authority that a few wrecked ships from the bottom of the river have been offered to the King – "lazy trades for pity pennies" mostly, nothing more than small fishing boats. In fact, I remember you telling me that some brave idiot had offered the King a kayak! I bet that went down a treat. I wonder, though, if it's the *Golden Hind*, if it's to be traded by someone . . . hmmmm.'

Edgar wasted no time in dispatching Claw to the King. 'Find out what's going on. If they are all on a quest to find the *Golden Hind*, I'll bet that the King knows about it.'

Claw left to discover all he could, even if he didn't relish the prospect of spending time below the

river with the fearsome
Crocodile King.

Edgar watched as the helpful
buck rat and his wife raced
through the thronging tourists at the Tower of
London and his thoughts turned to the *Golden Hind*.
A greedy urge for treasure made him shudder all over
with excitement.

Lupo could feel that his leg was getting worse. He
rubbed it with his nose and inspected the damage by
lowering the bandana. There was a slim splinter just
below the surface. As the others walked on, he took a
deep breath and then pulled out the piece of wood
with his teeth. Instantly, it felt better. Holly must
have seen that he had dropped back: she turned and
walked back towards him. Carefully and quickly, he
lifted the scarf to hide the wound.

Innocently, she said, 'Everything all right?'

'Yes, I'm good. It's a pretty amazing maze, huh?'
he said coolly, trying to distract her.

She smiled sweetly. 'It's something else. I hope
Herbert is keeping a note of all these wrong turns we
keep taking.'

Lupo hopped over to the mouse. 'Holly has just made a good point. How are we going to know exactly which is the right way?'

Herbert thought for a moment and then said, 'Of course!' He pulled out the golden thread Tommy had given him. Carefully, he tied the end of it to a stone on the ground. As he walked, he unwound the golden thread from the ball in his pocket. 'It's a marker. We can follow it back if we need to. This way we shall know if we are going round and round in circles.'

The maze was shifting, which meant that every now and then the high stone walls swivelled around. Herbert explained that it was the muddy cave. 'The stones are moving because of the floodwaters. It's as I said: we could lose the entire maze at any minute, so be on your guard!'

This didn't lift anyone's mood. They all were finding it hard enough to figure out their way around and now with the stones moving and falling it was a far from easy journey.

Kitty noticed that every corner was the same as the next and beyond every bend there was yet more stone. 'Will it ever end?' she pleaded. They hit as many dead paths as they did turnings. She had tried a couple of times to jump up over the stones, but they were too high even for her. Herbert could manage to get to the top, but he could see no clear route and only rows and rows of stone columns ahead. The maze was a puzzle all of them were trying to master.

'I don't understand. Why would someone want to build such a thing?' asked Kitty as she followed the thin golden thread as it wound its way around the walls.

'I've been thinking about who may have designed it and I have decided that this must have been the work of a master puzzle maker,' said Herbert.

'And someone with a lot of time on their hands,' added Holly.

Herbert agreed. 'Time and good ideas. This maze was designed to keep everyone out. A distraction, if you like, to stop the likes of us from finding the *Golden Hind*.'

Kitty sighed. 'I can imagine some human mapmaker spending hours deciding how he or she could keep us all permanently lost.'

Herbert shook his head. 'I'm not sure this

was a human's handiwork.'

Lupo asked, 'You think that all this could have been built and created by an animal?'

Herbert smiled. 'An animal who wanted to protect the *Golden Hind* and all the treasure.'

Lupo knew exactly who Herbert was talking about. 'You think that the lost pirate did this?'

Herbert nodded. 'It's entirely possible.'

Kitty shook her head. 'But that's crazy. You're saying Whisper the lost pirate built all this? A dog? I just don't know why you promised that ghost that you'd find her. She can't still be alive. She'd be hundreds of years old. I'm right, aren't I, Herbert?'

Herbert looked back at Kitty. 'Nothing is impossible.'

Lupo and Holly were enjoying spending the time together, even if it was far from the comfort of the palace. They were ahead of Herbert and Kitty, and deep in a conversation about Lupo's new life in Norfolk when they walked into the middle of the first of the maze's games.

It was Lupo who noticed that they were surrounded by large carved wooden horses. The horses were rearing up on their hind legs, threatening anyone who came too close.

'Now, this is very strange,' said Kitty. 'We walk around for ages and find nothing, and now we have lots of scary-looking wooden horses. Why are they here, Herbert?'

Herbert checked his notebook. 'This is the first of the maze's games. Be very careful, everyone. Like the Minotaurs, they may be booby-trapped.'

Kitty carried on walking forwards. Finding a pack of wooden playing cards on the floor, she picked them up. 'Hey, check these out! Cool!'

Unfortunately, she had managed to trigger the start of the game. The others barely got out of the way in time. The first horse slammed its front legs on to the ground and as it wound itself back up, a wooden card was left behind.

Holly looked nervous. 'Please tell me, Herbert, that we are not about to lose our heads.'

Herbert commanded everyone to stand very still. He studied the horses and Kitty's wooden playing cards. 'Very interesting,' he said, several times. 'I think that this is Snap. The bad news is that because Kitty triggered the start of the game she will have to play for us all. The rest of us should line up on the other side of the room.' Then something caught his eye unexpectedly. 'Unless someone has a key to that door.'

Behind the horses was a trapdoor that Vulcan had already spotted. He'd been using the golden thread to follow them around the maze. Much to his astonishment, none of them had noticed him. He slid into the darkness behind some horses and waited for the others to try to figure out the game.

Herbert studied the space in which they were all standing. He could see several trapdoors in the floor and behind them were some stone openings without keyholes. 'You see those stone doors?' He pointed and everyone nodded. 'Well, each of us must stand next to one of them. If Kitty wins the next round of Snap, we get to go on.'

Lupo looked at Kitty. 'And if she gets it wrong?'

Herbert shrugged. 'I think we will go flying down those trapdoors beneath the stone doors and I dread to think what's below us.'

Kitty sighed. 'What happens if I don't want to play?'

The stones around them began to move, closing around them and boxing them in with the horses and the wooden playing cards. All four of them rushed to try and find a way out but it was no good. They were trapped.

'I DON'T WANT TO PLAY!' screamed Kitty.

'Well, you have no choice. If you don't play, we end up stuck in here forever,' answered Herbert.

Lupo could see a large 'X' on the floor. 'I think that's where you have to stand, Kitty.'

Reluctantly Kitty went over to the large cross on the floor. 'Great, X marks the spot. Everyone ready?'

Holly, Lupo and Herbert each went and stood on top of the trapdoors next to the stone exits on the far side of the room. Herbert asked Kitty to tell them what the picture was on the first of her cards.

'It's kind of like a man in a hat with some swords and a K, I think.'

'It's a KING!' Holly cried out.

There was a small slot in the floor near the large X. Kitty could see that the card had to go into the slot. 'So now I just post it through the slot and hope for the best?'

Herbert asked, 'Now see what card the horse has. Is it a KING too?'

'YES, it's the same – so now what do I do?'

Holly and Lupo called out together, 'SNAP!'

Kitty posted the card through the slot and Holly's stone door opened so quickly that none of them had a chance to react. Holly was out and so was Vulcan.

Lupo sniffed her slab. 'HOLLY! CAN YOU HEAR US? HOLLY, WHERE ARE YOU?' But there was no answer. 'Kitty, carry on. You'd better hope that the next card is a snap or else I'm going to have to start trying to dig us out.'

The second horse reared up and the rider pushed forwards. The wooden horse crashed hard on to the soft ground with its wooden playing card.

Kitty looked for the card it left behind as it began to wind back up. 'It's a silly man with a funny face.'

Herbert said, 'It's a joker card. Kitty, what's your next card?'

'It's not the same. Mine is an eight of hearts with red roses. How odd.' As she posted it through the slot she said, 'It was a strange card. I don't think I have ever seen a playing card with roses twisted around it before!'

There was a rustling coming from somewhere in the room. Lupo readied himself.

Herbert felt the ground move. 'Oh no, something is coming.'

The room began to fill with the most beautiful hand-carved wooden roses. Kitty was lost in the magical splendour of the magnificent roses. So lost, she didn't see the twisted thorns that were headed in her direction.

'Kitty, watch out!' cried Lupo as the thorns twisted sharply towards the tabby's neck.

'How do we stop them?' she asked.

Herbert replied, 'We don't. We have to play on.'

Lupo felt dizzy. 'The roses are making us dizzy. Kitty, hurry.'

The roses with their sharp thorns were now all around Kitty. 'OK, I think I've got it. If I don't get a snap next these are going to kebab me!' She addressed the vicious plants which were closing in on her. 'Oh no, you stop right there. I'm not going to be a Kitty kebab!'

The next horse drew up and everyone got ready. Lupo knew that this was their last chance. The card it left behind was of a Queen. Kitty opened her eyes slowly, hoping that the card in her paw was the same.

'IT'S A QUEEN! We are saved!' She reached

through the thorns and posted the card. At the same moment, Herbert leapt on to Lupo's back and the two of them fell through the stone door.

Lupo opened his eyes to see Holly wagging her tail. He felt his heart beating faster as she ran over to them. 'Lupo! Herbert! You're OK! But where's Kitty?'

They all waited, looking around for another door to open. But Kitty never came.

Lupo picked himself up off the floor. 'We have to move on. It's the only way to free her. Don't you see? We need to finish the maze.'

Holly began to panic. 'We can't leave her behind. What if something happens, what if—'

Herbert agreed. 'Lupo's right, Holly. We have to get going. It's the only way to save her now.'

12
Pythons and Staircases

They agreed that the only thing they could do was carry on in the hope that Kitty would be freed once they had found their way out. All of them now felt a need to hurry.

Herbert retied the golden thread, and pulled out his notebook. 'I don't think it will be the last of the games. Sir Francis warned me that the maze will present us with a new game when it's ready. He told me to be prepared at any time. We must pass all the games to get out of the maze. I think we should stop and have a rest now so that I can try and work out what others we can expect. Cheese sandwich, anyone?'

Lupo had fallen through the stone doorway. His poorly leg was now throbbing. Holly sniffed the bandana around it and knew that Lupo had to be in

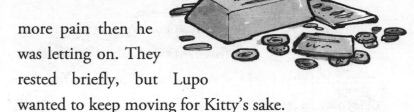

more pain then he
was letting on. They
rested briefly, but Lupo
wanted to keep moving for Kitty's sake.

Herbert thought he had figured out what game
may come next but didn't want to scare them.
Instead, he sang what he thought was Lupo's pirate
song quietly as they walked. 'A sailor's life for
me . . . All at sea . . . All at sea.'

They had been walking for a while. All the stones
around them looked the same. Nothing was changing.
By the third wrong turn into a dead end, Holly felt
that Lupo badly needed a break. 'Herbert, I think we
need to rest again. We aren't getting anywhere and
I'm worried about Lupo's leg.'

Lupo kept walking. 'No, we can't stop. Kitty is all
alone in those thorns and she needs us to carry on.'
He was determined not to let Kitty down.

All three of them arrived at the next room.
None of them was happy about having to face
another game.

The room was bigger this time and there was a
staircase leaning against a wall with three holes in
it. To Lupo, the game looked like George and

Charlotte's Snakes and Ladders and he dared not say anything for fear that it was exactly that. So they stood looking at the stairs and the holes, waiting for Herbert to speak.

Eventually, Herbert ran on to the staircase to get a better look. And the very second his paw hit the first step, the stone walls began closing in around them.

'Oh no, not again!' shouted Holly.

'Now I play,' said Herbert as he moved confidently up the stairs to start the game. He stopped at the top. From high up he saw doors hidden in the stones. 'Go over to those stones; those are the doors out. Hopefully this time we will all make it through.'

Lupo and Holly moved to the stones and waited. Once everyone was ready, he put his paw into the first hole. 'There is something here,' he said as he picked the object up and pulled it out. It was a pretty clockwork doll. 'Now, I wasn't expecting that!' he said.

Holly suggested that they wind the doll up to see what happened. Lupo agreed. 'It might be a clue?'

Delicately Herbert wound up the toy doll. The doll's eyes opened and then out of its mouth popped a note written on old faded paper.

Don't get bit!
An offering in payment will settle the debt.
Pay or you wilt not go on your way!

Holly's pretty blue eyes read and reread the paper. 'It's the same paper and handwriting as the note we found in the wooden dog. At least we know we are on the right track. "Don't get bit"? That could mean that inside those holes in front of you there could be something that could bite. Herbert, please be careful.'

Herbert was feeling queasy. He had failed to calculate the consequences of his action, and now he was on top of a staircase about to get eaten. His notebook didn't mention anything about being bitten but it did warn him to expect a snake. He made a promise to himself then and there that if he ever got out of the maze he would ask Issy the mouse to marry him.

A smudge on his glasses distracted him. He wiped it away with his pocket handkerchief and thought it best to try and stay focused on the task in hand, pushing all thoughts of the red mouse in a wedding dress out of his mind. 'Concentrate, Herbert!' he muttered to himself.

'Payment? Of a debt?' Lupo thought long and hard.

Herbert came up with the answer. 'Quick, Holly, pass me the buttons you bought!'

Holly passed the royal spaniel the three buttons she had found in the night market. 'Why buttons?'

Herbert jumped up and down in excitement. 'Quite brilliant! Of course we can use the buttons as payment of the debt!'

Lupo threw the buttons up to him, one by one. Before they could finish congratulating themselves on working out the clue, the game had begun. The staircase creaked towards the first hole.

It was a small, round hole. Herbert was clutching the buttons against his chest. He could feel his heart beating faster and faster.

'Right. Here I go. I'm going to put the first button in the hole and see what happens.'

'Good luck, Herbert!' shouted Holly. 'You'll be fine.'

The brown mouse eased the button into the hole and waited. Nothing happened. He looked, bewildered, back at his friends. 'Nothing?'

Vulcan could see exactly what was about to happen. From where he was standing he could see a large python slithering out of another hole. It was moving very slowly. And staying hidden from Herbert. When it got to the bottom of the staircase, it wrapped its long thin body around and around. It then started to curl its way up towards Herbert who couldn't see the danger he was in.

But Holly and Lupo saw the snake. 'HERBERT! SNAKE!' they shouted.

'I don't understand? I paid the debt?' questioned Herbert.

The python was almost to the top of the stairs when the staircase moved on to the next hole. Herbert instantly began descending the stairs. He narrowly missed the poisonous snake as it slithered past him and disappeared into the top hole, taking the clockwork doll with it.

The first door opened and Holly was out. Vulcan dived in after her but barely made it through without being seen. He rolled away from her as the door slammed shut, thinking, 'Two games down, two to go; see you on the other side, Lupo.'

'Pay the debt, Herbert, and let's get out of here!' said Lupo.

Herbert clung on to the buttons tightly. 'One moment. I need to say something. Whatever happens, you must push on. Get to the end of the maze.'

Lupo nodded. 'You're coming with us. Throw the button then run over here. We are all getting out this time.'

Herbert threw the button into the middle hole. But missed it. Lupo turned to see if the doors were opening. As they did, Herbert saw the python. The Head of MI5 had no choice but to dive into the middle hole.

The last thing Lupo saw was Herbert running into the hole with his last button. The python was right behind him. With the debt paid, the doors opened and Holly pulled Lupo through. The door crashed closed and Herbert, like Kitty, was stranded on the other side.

Lupo barked loudly. 'This is a nightmare! Now we've lost Herbert.'

Holly touched Lupo's paw. 'He'll be all right. Come on,

we need to move on. Finish the maze and find them.'

Lupo knew that they had no choice. She was right. They both took in their new surroundings. Only they weren't in a stone maze any more. They were both standing in a luscious green jungle.

Ebony and her crew had brazenly crushed several animals' attempts to escape the rising flood waters. 'OUT OF MY WAY' she had commanded, and the poor animals fled for safety. She had managed to get to the very edge of Kensington Palace and – just as the map had indicated – there was a narrow tunnel big enough for animals only. 'This is it – we have made it to the Red route.' She smugly marvelled at the thought that the *Golden Hind* had been within touching distance of the royal palace for all this time. No one but her knew.

Chump spoke up. 'I've always wanted to visit Kensington Palace. What about you, Lump?'

The lizard's eyes swivelled in their sockets. 'Wait till the hive hears we got to travel along the Red route. They'll be well impressed!'

Ebony turned to face her crew. 'Now, listen up, you lot! Once we are in, we need to move fast. This is my treasure and I won't have it snatched from my claws by anyone – least of all some meddling royal pet!' Ebony studied the map and she walked into the tunnel, 'To the gold!' she cried. 'We are looking for a tapestry which shows the ship. FIND IT!'

Chump the crocodile looked around the narrow tunnel and complained. 'But every picture on the wall is of an animal. I don't see any ships!'

Lump squirmed along the red-carpeted route. 'Nice and warm down here. Luxury! I think I might . . . Hang on – that's a ship.'

Ebony ran to his side. The lizard was standing in front of Tommy's newly repaired tapestry. 'Well done, Lump. You found it. That has to be it!' She flicked out her sharp claws and ran them down the length of the fine tapestry, ripping the priceless work to ribbons. 'Oops! My bad,' she said mercilessly. A cold breeze blew through the shredded picture. Her crew rubbed their paws together, hungry for gold. Ebony smiled, 'Like I said, good things come to those who wait.'

'My scales are drying out,' grumbled Chump, who was badly in need of a good soak. 'Will there be water around the ship?'

'This is no time for baths. We have work to do. We need to get the treasure and get out!' Ebony replied impatiently. Two cats that liked to think they were her personal guards stepped in through the damaged tapestry. Ebony watched them. 'This is it, boys – well done. Now it's a simple plan. Remove all the golden treasure, then hide it. I plan on trading the ship with your filthy smelly master.'

Chump sighed. 'I miss the Crocodile King. The hive is ever so nice now that he's finished it.'

'Well, hurry up and get going,' meowed Ebony. 'The sooner we get that gold the sooner you'll be back under the Thames! And one more thing. After we are done with the *Golden Hind*, I want a list of every secret royal passage. I need access to all the royal households and I'm betting there are passages like the Red route under them all.'

The stones within the previous part of the maze were nothing like the thick jungle Holly and Lupo found they now had to navigate. They walked for a while before remembering to use Herbert's ball of golden thread. Holly was sure that they had walked certain paths before.

After a brief stop to check on Lupo's leg, they were off again and it wasn't too long before they found themselves in another maze game. Lupo was on his guard. 'Be careful, Holly.'

It was not like the other games. Firstly, it looked very much out of place in the middle of the dense green jungle because it was a bedroom. Everything was beautifully arranged. There was a bed and some chairs, all covered in the finest of silks. Holly pointed up to the trees. 'Look at the mirrors, Lupo, there are so many of them!' The mirrors hung on every tree around the bed and chairs.

Lupo looked puzzled. 'What a strange place. It's nothing like the other games. What do you think we have to do?'

Holly agreed. 'I've never seen so many mirrors all in one place.' She studied a large portrait of Queen Elizabeth I. The Tudor queen was wearing a big dress and on her head was a crown. In her hand she held a tiny golden deer. 'The deer is important, of that I am sure. Can you see the way she's holding it so high up, as if it sits with her crown.'

Lupo dared not move a muscle. He knew that this

was one of the maze's tricks. 'Herbert called the ship the *Golden Hind*. You don't think the two are related?'

'Yes, of course, a hind is a female deer! I think that she is holding it so high because it meant a great deal to her. Lupo, we must be so close! This has to be the final clue to finding the ship.' Holly ran around the room, looking for more evidence.

'Holly, wait! Stop!' Lupo called out, but he was too late.

The final challenge had begun. On a bed in the corner of the room a wooden woman began to rise. Holly instantly barked; Lupo growled. The woman was dressed as Queen Elizabeth I. She even had long, red curly hair that was the same as the great Queen's.

Lupo could hear the ropes around the room moving the wooden figure towards Holly. Not for the first time that day he suspected someone was keeping a close eye on them. He whispered to Holly. 'That's odd, can you hear the ropes and pulleys? Someone has to be moving everything.'

Holly didn't have a chance to agree. The wooden Queen stood in front of the royal dog. She stared down and a voice boomed out around the room. 'PLAY OR DIE!'

There was no way out. The jungle had closed in around them. Holly replied to the wooden Queen in a nervous voice. 'What is the game, Your Royal Highness?'

'MIRROR, MIRROR.'

It was not a game Lupo knew how to play but Holly's tail was wagging: a good sign she was happy. 'I can do this!' she said confidently.

Lupo fought his way through the thick branches of a tree and discovered a doorway. 'I think I have found the way out. If you play the game and get stuck I will do my best to find the ship and stop whoever is to blame for all of this, Holly. I'll get you and the others back. I promise.'

Holly was smiling. 'I know you will. This is easy! I'll see you on the other side. I'm going to need that pocket mirror we bought in the market. Throw it over to me and you go and wait by the door. Remember to jump out the minute you can. I'll be fine.'

Lupo nodded and pulled the mirror out from within the bandana. 'Here, catch,' he said, skimming it along the floor into her open paws.

146

'Thanks!' she said.

'Are you ready?'

Lupo pushed on the door in front of him. It was firmly closed. 'As I'll ever be!'

The wooden Queen moved around the room and looked into every mirror, asking it the same question. 'WHO IS THE MOST BEAUTIFUL OF THEM ALL?'

Each time Holly would answer, 'You are, my Queen.'

The wooden Queen then made her way over to Holly and stopped. She lowered her wooden body so that she was looking directly into Holly's pretty blue eyes.

'MIRROR, MIRROR, WHO IS THE MOST BEAUTIFUL OF THEM ALL?' asked the Queen.

For a moment, Holly was confused. She looked behind her to see if there was a mirror but there wasn't. Holly had a thought: 'It's my eyes. She can see herself in my eyes. This is a trick!'

'Be careful, Holly,' Lupo warned. 'Look around for anything that can catch you out before you answer.'

He was right to be concerned. Holly could feel a draught coming up from the floor under her feet. She looked down briefly and could see that she was standing on a trapdoor. She also knew that the very minute she answered, the door would open and she would fall downwards.

Holly breathed in deeply and then out again before lifting up the pocket mirror from the market. The wooden Queen was staring at her own reflection in the mirror.

'See, you're nothing but a wooden toy!' Holly cried out.

A voice full of rage filled the room. 'HOW DARE YOU RUIN MY GAME!'

Both the trapdoors opened. Lupo jumped through his, but Holly wasn't quick enough. As she fell, she saw Vulcan in the pocket mirror stepping out of the room. She barked as loudly as she could, 'LUPO! VULCAN!' Then, she, like Kitty and Herbert, was gone.

13
The Golden Hind

Lupo was alone. He had heard Holly calling out his name as she had fallen through the trapdoor. There was nothing he could have done to help her. He thought of the royal children in the nursery and wanted to go home, but he knew he had to rescue his friends: no amount of treasure was worth losing his friend and his family for. Looking around him, he realised he had no choice but to continue onwards. Fortunately, his leg was feeling a bit stronger. He tied what remained of the golden thread to some overgrown bushes and started to walk.

The air in the maze was thicker and he could feel warmth coming from nearby. At least he was out of the jungle. He watched as stones shifted in front of him and an opening was revealed. He walked through, sniffing the air for clues. He was sure he could smell a roasting fire. He said aloud, 'Now that's all I need, my nose is tricking me!' A yawn escaped him and he tried to shake off any feeling of tiredness. Kitty, Herbert and Holly all needed him to stay awake.

His head fell heavily when he saw the thin golden thread on the floor. He had been going around in circles. He couldn't afford to make any more mistakes. He set off again, only to end up back at the same bushes once again. The golden thread was exactly where it had always been.

'ENOUGH!' he barked. 'No more games. I need to help my friends. I have to find a way out of here.'

He then remembered what the three blind mice had told him. 'Use your senses!' He decided to trust his nose and follow the scent of the fire. The only problem was that the trail ended at the same point every time. Lupo sat down to think and found he was looking at a large stone in front of him. 'Well,' he thought to himself, 'the entire maze had been full of tricks. Maybe this is a trick stone wall?'

He stood up, and walked over to the wall. He

pushed hard against it. 'Here goes everything!' he said aloud, and jumped as heavily as he could on the stone.

The stone opened and he fell on to the hard floor below, landing quickly with a bump. Rubbing his sore leg, he inhaled deeply. 'The fire is closer. I can smell the wood burning now!' Following his nose, he walked into a stone cavern. He could just make out a light up ahead.

He felt his paws wanting to move faster, so he began to run towards the light. As the cavern opened up to a much larger cave, he came to a skidding halt. In front of him was a huge golden pirate ship with a giant red deer painted on its enormous sails.

Lupo was so excited, he leapt high in the air. 'It's here! I've found it! THE *GOLDEN HIND*!'

Lupo's happiness was short-lived. Another dog walked out of the shadows. 'Yes, you have, but it was such a shame you had to lose all of your friends along the way, Lupo.'

Lupo snarled, 'VULCAN.'

Vulcan pushed past. 'Enough of the pleasantries, I think. I don't know about you, but I am looking forward to seeing all my treasure.'

Lupo watched as Vulcan began to walk up a gangway leading to the main deck of the pirate ship.

Vulcan looked down at Lupo, 'Oh I almost forgot. Here boy, FETCH!' Herbert's ball of golden thread flew through the air and landed next to Lupo's sore paw.

Vulcan had used the thread to follow them through the maze. With the thread gone, they would never be able to find their way out again.

'You took the thread!' cried Lupo. 'Now how do we get out? Vulcan, you have trapped us all with your selfishness.'

Vulcan laughed. 'That was my plan. I hope you don't disappoint me. I'd hate to see you again.'

Vulcan carried on climbing higher. Lupo raced up the gangway until he had caught up with him. They both pushed on, equally determined to make it on to the main deck first.

In the end it was Lupo who was first on board. With as much revulsion as he could convey, he asked, 'How could you watch us all sacrifice ourselves to get here and not say anything?'

'Calm yourself. I found it all rather enjoyable. Seeing your friends captured while you pushed on so bravely, leaving all your friends behind. It was quite special really. Now who's the bad dog?'

Lupo growled but he knew Vulcan was right. He had failed his friends.

'I didn't see you trying to stop them. Or even turn back,' continued Vulcan, pushing and prodding at Lupo's guilty feelings.

Lupo's ears dropped low. There was little defence he could muster.

Vulcan had the upper hand now, and he knew it. 'I will need you to help carry all my treasure, so I suggest you help me find it. Then I can get out of here.'

'How?' Lupo asked, throwing the ball of golden thread back at Vulcan. 'You took away your best hope of getting back when you stole the thread!'

It was a moment for Vulcan to savour. 'Oh Lupo, when will you learn? You don't think I would come all the way down here without a plan to get out, do you? Come, come. I thought you knew me better than that. Ebony is on her way: through the secret entrance!'

Lupo's ears lifted with curiosity. 'Ebony! I don't understand. Did you plan this together?'

Vulcan swaggered around on the fabulous old ship. 'You can't have believed that you were the only ones with clues to the whereabouts of the *Golden Hind*?'

Lupo shook his head. 'But how did you find out? I mean, what clues did you have?'

The Queen's dorgi contemplated telling Lupo everything and then thought better of it. This time, the royal spaniel would have no chances to wreck Vulcan's plans.

'If I were you, I would be more concerned about your friends right now,' he said. 'I wouldn't be surprised if Ebony has already found the treasure. You see, Lupo, that's what everyone is after. *We* will find it and then we will find the passageway that leads us out – leaving you behind to be washed away with the floodwaters.' Lupo growled.

'WHO ARE YOU?' said a voice from behind them both. 'What are you doing on my ship?'

Lupo and Vulcan turned around to see a grey dog in a black pirate hat. 'Whisper, the lost pirate!' Lupo exclaimed in amazement.

Ebony watched as Lump the lizard climbed out last on to the lower deck of the impressive *Golden Hind*.

As her green eyes danced over the beautiful ship, she felt a sudden surge of sadness. In some way, it reminded her of the vast fleet of boats she had once commanded in ancient Egypt. Her ships, like this one, had stood strong and proud.

The *Golden Hind* was very different, though. On closer inspection she found that this ship was far larger than even her most impressive vessel.

Chump was hungry. He snapped his jaws as they walked around. When he saw a sign indicating the way to the ship's galley kitchen, he suggested that they all go and take a look. 'There might be some goodies!' he said.

The cats guarding Ebony whispered amongst themselves. 'Like there will be anything good still worth eating on a 400-year-old ship!' They fell about laughing at the crocodile's stupidity but stopped abruptly when they felt Ebony's icy glare on them.

The galley was surprisingly clean. Stuffed birds and bones of dead animals all hung from hooks above a warm stove. Copper cups and smashed plates had been tossed into a barrel, which overflowed with knives and forks. Maggots wriggled along the woodwork tops and fell on to the damp and dusty floor.

'There is nothing here!' said Chump, flicking his tail restlessly.

Ebony stood perfectly still. 'Shhhh, Chump. Who lit the stove? It's warm. That must mean that we are not alone on this ship. Someone else is here.'

None of the crew of misfit animals said a word.

'By the look of this galley they have been down here for some time. You two,' she pointed to her cats, 'go ahead, quietly. And keep your eyes open for someone, or something.' She double-checked her map. 'The map says the treasure is downstairs and round the next corner.'

Neither Vulcan nor Lupo could believe their eyes. Standing on the upper deck of the ship was a shaggy lurcher dog. Its messy fur was a dusty grey and it wore a black pirate's hat and a reddish leather collar. This bore the seal of Queen Elizabeth I. Both Vulcan and Lupo watched as it pointed a sword in their direction.

The grey dog took her time looking over the visitors. 'You looked smaller in the maze.' She spoke in a soft, raspy voice. 'Still, you made it out, so you must be worth holding on to. Now who are you both and what are you doing here?' she demanded, thrusting her sword in their faces.

Bravely Lupo stepped forward. 'I am Lupo and this is Vulcan. I'm looking for my friends who were taken in the maze.' He got the feeling that the grey dog was more interested in Vulcan.

'So, you came for my treasure?' She aimed her sword at the royal dorgi.

Vulcan felt the icy blade resting on his throat. 'You're a female. How quaint: a female pirate dog. Remove the blade from my neck immediately!'

The pirate dog wasn't about to back down. Lupo watched as the two dogs growled viciously at each other.

'Please stop. Please. If you let us go, we will leave. We don't want the treasure. I just want my friends back. Please.' Lupo looked at the sharp sword as the cool blade twisted against Vulcan's neck. 'Wait!'

'Why do you care?' answered the pirate dog. 'You are only here for my treasure and besides, this dog has been following you since the start. He is no friend of yours. I watched him use you all.'

Lupo wasn't about to give up. 'You're right. He is no friend of mine, but you have no reason to hurt him. We haven't done anything apart from finding our way on to your ship. Please.'

The pirate dog lowered her sword whilst keeping her copper brown eyes trained on the two strange dogs. 'You are both trespassing. I don't trust this one.' She pointed her sword at Vulcan. 'As for you, Lupo, I congratulate you in succeeding where so many humans have failed. It will be a shame to have to get rid of you; it has been a very long time since I have had company. But I am duty bound to protect this ship and its contents. Vulcan must die.'

Lupo stepped forwards. 'We mean you no harm, so please put the sword away.' He looked into the grey dog's eyes softly. 'I don't suppose it would be all right if we got some water? Only it's been a long journey and . . .'

'The only water you'll be enjoying today will be the water beneath the plank. So walk the plank, you two!' She took the sword from Vulcan's neck and pointed it towards a wooden beam at the end of the ship.

Vulcan stepped away, but suddenly he felt the end of her blade once again. It was now resting against his ribs. 'Excuse me, Miss. Now, that really doesn't work for me. I'm afraid of heights, you see and . . .'

She forced them both over to the plank. They were both about to be tossed overboard.

Lupo could think of only one way out of the tricky situation they found themselves in. 'Look – no need to push him – it's OK. I understand what it's like to want to protect your family. Vulcan and I will both jump.'

'We will?' asked Vulcan.

Whisper's blade was forcing them both towards the end of the plank. Two more steps and they would both be in the muddy floodwaters below. Lupo could feel his sore paw throbbing and yet all he could think of was his friends. 'Yes, Vulcan, we can jump. But first could you at least tell me if my friends are all right?'

Whisper poked both of them harder with the tip of her sword. 'What do you care? You left them, didn't you?' She swung her sword in the direction of the enormous maze. 'In there. I saw you.'

Lupo quickly turned around so that he was face to face with Whisper the pirate. 'Yes, you're right, but you are also wrong. You see, I made a mistake. I shouldn't have convinced them to come with me in the first place. They are more than just my friends: they are part of my family.'

Whisper whistled. 'Aren't you a big softy? Since you seem like the real deal, I'll challenge you to a sword fight for them.'

Lupo felt a rush of joy. 'They are all right?'

Vulcan groaned. 'Oh please! Someone push me off.'

Whisper handed Lupo a sword. 'Your friends are down in the cells. Fight me for them!'

Lupo grabbed the sword and aimed it at Whisper. The lurcher was quick on her feet. She darted from one end of the magnificent ship to the other. Lupo was trying his best to keep up. He had to tuck his head to avoid being swiped on the left and then on the right.

'You're pretty good at this but not as good as me!' mocked Whisper.

Lupo lunged forwards, catching Whisper unawares. She reached out and grabbed a rope on the

side of the mast,
but Lupo copied
her movement and in a
flash they were both flying through the air, charging
at each other with their swords held aloft. Lupo
found his strength and swung on to the mast. Then
he pulled hard on Whisper's rope and she came
clattering down on to the deck.

'Yikes!' she cried, jumping back up. 'That was
close.'

Lupo suddenly knocked over a barrel, which
rolled down the deck making a sound like thunder.
'Watch out, Vulcan!' he barked.

Whisper had no choice but to try and jump over
it. He marvelled as the pirate dog flew clean over the
thundering barrel.

As she fought, she found she was enjoying herself.
It had been many years since she had met someone
who could fight so well.

Lupo saw his opportunity and ran around the
back of the ship. He then caught Whisper, slipping
the sword right in front of her. 'I win!' he exclaimed.

Whisper was so out of breath, she simply laughed.
'OK! You win!' But his victory was short-lived.

Vulcan had gone, and moments later he was on deck with Kitty, Herbert and Holly.

Lupo's tail wagged – he was really thrilled to see his friends all safe and well.

Vulcan had chained them all together. Under his arm was a stick of dynamite. 'When you two have quite finished playing perhaps we could all go and find my treasure or I'll blow up the whole ship – and Lupo, you'll never see your friends or family ever again.'

14
Gold Fever

Ebony was below decks. The ship was in a bad way; it creaked like it was cracking from the inside out. In the sleeping quarters, she pushed skeletons out of their hammocks, exclaiming, 'What good are sleeping skeletons and look at all this junk!'

There were pictures of sailors with their families, hand-carved boards game and bits of uniform littering the walls and floors. Candle-wax drippings stained most of the blackened columns within the sleeping quarters. It was as if the entire room had been left ready for the sailors' departure. Only they had never left.

'What happened to them?' asked one of the cats.

Ebony twirled her tail around a skeleton's ribcage. 'Mutiny. These humans thought they could steal the treasure away, hide out and wait for the tide to turn in their favour. Trouble was, they would have starved to death in this cave.'

'I think I've found something,' said Lump the lizard, who was looking inside an old chest.

Ebony peered into the leather box. 'Yes, you have. You cats can go down these secret stairs first. I don't want any surprises. The treasure is almost in my reach. I can feel it.'

Lupo was trying to get a good look at the ropes and chains that Whisper had used to tie his friends together. Herbert was unusually quiet. Lupo could see that his little paws were bound together from behind with a good sailors' knot. Holly smiled sweetly at him but he could tell she was very uncomfortable, chained to Kitty by her collar.

Kitty hadn't stopped talking. 'Can you at least try taking the collar off? I mean, where am I going to go? Where are any of us going? We're all stuck down here together and the only way out is lost. No thanks to that crazy dog,' she said, pulling her head towards Vulcan. 'Oh, and did I forget to mention he's planning on blowing us all up!?'

Whisper wasn't used to being ordered around on her own ship. She was without her sword but felt completely unafraid. Fearlessly, she charged at Vulcan as he attempted to tie Lupo up. 'Let him go!' she demanded. 'These are my prisoners.'

'No. Get down those stairs, the miserable lot of you,' Vulcan ordered.

As the group began to descend, the deck of the magnificent ship was pelted by falling stones. The cave around the ship was crumbling fast.

Herbert inspected one of the stones that landed on the stair in front of him. 'It's mud. Not stone at all,' he told Holly.

'Mud? Really?' Holly asked, surprised.

Speaking in a hushed voice so that only Holly could hear, Herbert said, 'Geologically you would term this as clay. Either way, this explains why the ship has been so well preserved. It also means that the cave could collapse at any moment. If the storm causes the clay to get wet enough, it could very well fall in on itself. I fear we are running out of time.'

Holly leaned towards the smartest mouse in the country and asked, 'Since you are so very clever, would you mind explaining to me exactly how we

would survive, if the cave collapsed. I'm sure we would break up like a toothpick: it's just not exactly the safest of ships to be stuck in if the walls come crashing down.'

Whisper was taking them to the treasure. Since the unexpected visitors had no way out, she was confident they would be stuck down here with her.

Earlier, she had received a visit from the ghostly Queen Elizabeth I who said that King Henry VIII was hosting a ball in his palace at Hampton Court and that they would be bringing a number of guests down to the ship, to show off the splendid royal treasure. Whisper was confident that the dogs would be so frightened of the spirits that she would get her opportunity to seize them as her prisoners. The only problem was that the cave was now disappearing. It had been so many years since she had seen daylight and part of her was looking forward to it all falling in. Perhaps then she would smell the sea air once more.

They were standing in an empty room. Vulcan was agitated and demanding to know where the treasure was hidden. 'Stop wasting my time. Where is it all, you filthy pirate?' he said, threatening Whisper with her own sword.

'Yes.' Ebony was there, surrounded by her mob. 'Why don't you be a darling and take us all to the treasure?'

Whisper had spent her life guarding the treasure and she would die protecting it, if she had to. That was the oath she had sworn to her beloved Captain before he had left.

She had come on board with the ship's carpenter as a young pup and had grown up on the seas, chasing rats from the galley and comforting the sailors. It had been a tough life but she had loved every minute of it. She had fond memories of clear, calm nights when she could look overboard and watch the ocean coming alive beneath her. There was nothing as magical to her as looking up and seeing the night sky covered in a thousand twinkling stars. To a dog pirate there was nothing more wondrous.

She was well aware that the humans she worked for craved jewels more precious than the stars. They hungered for gold, and, more particularly, Spanish gold.

Life on the British shores was not easy back in Tudor times. The young Queen Elizabeth

I had inherited an empty treasury. Strife and hunger were part of everyday life. When the Queen ordered that the *Golden Hind* be sent to work to find the riches needed to save England, Whisper found herself sailing into unchartered waters. It hadn't been easy watching the desperate sailors' faces as they searched in vain for gold. Years went by before the day finally came.

Now Whisper had no choice but to give in and show where the treasure was kept. As she took Lupo and his friends, and Vulcan and Ebony's crew down to the bottom of the ship, she recalled that awful day when they had found the *Golden Hind*'s cursed hoard.

'You should know that this is no ordinary treasure,' Whisper said, pointing to the far corner of the ship. 'It all started when we spotted an island. Out at sea you could go for months and not see an inhabited island. But when the chef needed supplies and there was a sickness on board, we decided to go to the island to pick up crew and supplies, only we got more than we bargained for.'

Lupo and his friends were listening to the brave pirate as Vulcan and Ebony walked behind, looking in cupboards and boxes for any sign of the treasure.

'You won't find it in those,' she called back. 'The treasure you seek is so precious only one member of the crew was allowed the key to keep it safe.'

'Who was that?' Holly asked.

'The bravest man on the ship was not the captain but a young boy. He was a stowaway, of course, but he was a nice enough and a useful kind of kid. We would get him to climb up the mast in big storms and guide us through rocky waters. His name was Wolfe. On the day that we landed on the island, Wolfe took off like a shot. Since I was pretty young back then too, I went with him everywhere. I liked the boy; he taught me how to fight with a sword!

'While the rest of the crew went off to find supplies and crew, Wolfe and I went to explore the island. Let me tell you, finding my land legs wasn't easy but I got there eventually and when I did, we ran all over the island. We found flightless birds with legs as long as any horses running wild. Wolfe and I knew that they would make ideal food for the ship but catching them was hard! Eventually we managed to catch a few, just before the local farmer warned us to stay away from the home of the strange birds. He wouldn't say why, only that it was a cursed place.

'The Captain listened to Wolfe when he explained all that we had seen. Then he said we must all go to the birds' nesting ground. If only I had tried harder to stop it.'

Whisper looked fearful but continued. 'The nest was on the top of a cave not unlike this one. Never in all my long life had I feasted on so many eggs and chewed on so much sugar cane! But the cave collapsed. We fell in along with the nests. In the pit of that cave we found this . . .'

Whisper was standing by a door. She reached into a barrel by the side of it and removed a gold key. It shone in the soft warm yellow torchlight. Impatiently, Vulcan pushed past Whisper and opened the door and there gleamed the treasure they had all come to see.

Ebony and Vulcan rushed in to take a better look at the gold and silver, jewels and precious stones that the pirates had collected.

Lupo could see a flicker of something strange in Whisper's eye. He nudged Herbert in order to stop him

and the others from going inside.

'Look at Whisper. She's crying,' Lupo said to Herbert.

A single tear fell from the dog's face. 'Enjoy it while you can, because this treasure is cursed. The farmer on the island was right,' she said as she pushed Lupo and his friends out of the door and slammed it shut.

Ebony, Vulcan and the others remained trapped inside.

Whisper untied Herbert and said, 'I'm sorry, I was wrong about you all. I'll show you the way out.'

Herbert ran to the pirate dog's side. 'What happened to Wolfe and what is the curse?'

Whisper wiped away her tear and then cleared her throat. 'Wolfe, like the rest of them, got the gold fever.'

Holly shook her head. 'What's that?'

'I watched the humans become so obsessed with the rich stuff that they forgot to take care of themselves. They fought the captain and took over the ship. They locked us all in his cabin while they gorged themselves on gold, celebrating their loathsome victory. But they ran though the rations too quickly. They were more interested in their victory than taking care of the ship. As food and water ran out, they all began to die. The Captain and Wolfe were barely alive when the few remaining crew members begged for forgiveness and for the maps that could steer us all home. We were heroes when we got back, but in taking the gold we had all paid a heavy price. The Captain made the Queen promise that the *Golden Hind* would be kept hidden and the gold locked away so that no one else would suffer gold fever.

'Wolfe and I stayed down here guarding the ship and together we built the maze to protect the *Golden Hind* and the terrible treasure. Wolfe eventually grew up and he too became lost in the shimmering of the gold. When we lost sight of the twinkling stars above, he left. One day, my captain will return, and then I will be free.'

Lupo, Kitty, Holly and Herbert all looked at each other. They had found Sir Francis's dog.

A rumbling below decks stopped them all. A large part of the cave around them had collapsed and the entire ship rocked uneasily to the left and then to the right, throwing them all off their paws.

Kitty meowed, 'Great. If we are not trapped by the falling cave we get to suffer gold fever. Will someone get me out of here? NOW!'

15
Trapped

Whisper rushed Lupo and his friends to the Captain's cabin. 'The secret exit is this way,' she told them.

The Captain's cabin was by far the finest room on the ship. When Lupo walked in, it felt like he had slipped into another time. Pictures of Queen Elizabeth I hung at either end of the room. There was a large four-poster feather bed with heavy red velvet curtains, and all around the room ran a shelf with various kinds of books and objects. From the look of it, the Captain had left his clothing chest behind.

'I don't understand. It's blocked!' cried Whisper as she tried to force open a secret doorway out of the *Golden Hind*.

'It's the cave. It has fallen in and sealed the way

closed. We can't get out this way – the only exit is back through the maze!' he told the others.

Kitty was feeling sick. She needed air. Lupo offered to walk her up to the main deck.

'You go on deck, Lupo. I'll stay here and see if I can help find us another way out,' Holly said.

Herbert was too busy frantically throwing the maps around to see the others leaving.

Back on the deck Lupo made sure Kitty was comfortable. 'Sea sick, huh?'

'Yup!' said Kitty curling her tail back and forth. 'Errrr, yuck . . .'

There was another rumbling. Large clay stones rained down on the deck, punching holes in the ship's sails as they passed. When a very large bit of the cave came crashing down and Lupo had to dive to save Kitty, he knew that they were out of time. 'This cave isn't going to hold up much longer. We really need a way out.' But just as he finished speaking, water began pouring into the cave. The *Golden Hind* rocked heavily to one side.

As Kitty was pulled to the other side of the enormous ship, she dug her claws into the soft wood to stop herself from falling. Lupo caught a rope

as it swung by and
with a bit of quick
thinking, he was able
to tie the rope around his paw and swing over to
catch Kitty.

There was a loud bang and more water poured
into the cave. The ship stopped rocking just long
enough for Lupo and Kitty to drop back down on
to the deck and race back below to the Captain's
cabin. He barked loudly to his friends, 'The cave is
crumbling and water is pouring in. We don't have
long. Grab the maps; we have to set the others free.
It won't be long before this whole place will be
under water.'

Reluctantly, Whisper agreed to set the others free.
'Fine, but I've seen it before. Once they've had a
whiff of that gold, they won't want to leave.'

Lupo went with her to free Ebony and Vulcan,
whilst the others tried their best to grab as many
maps as they could.

Ebony was furious when Lupo and Whisper
opened the door. 'What are you playing at locking us
in here? Get out of the way. Chump, put as much
gold as you can into those empty barrels, the rest of

you can help him. Vulcan, get to work!' she ordered.

Lupo could see that Vulcan had the fever. He could see the look of longing and love the dorgi had for the forsaken treasure. Even though every hair on his body was telling him not to go in, Lupo ran into the room. He grabbed at the royal dorgi. 'Vulcan, snap out of it. There isn't time. The cave, it's . . .'

Vulcan growled viciously. 'Get away from me and my gold.'

'Please, Vulcan, please.' Lupo was trying desperately to pull him out of the room. They were right by the door when Vulcan swung around.

This time Vulcan bared his crooked teeth. 'This is *my* gold,' he said coldly.

Whisper reached in and pulled Lupo away. 'Leave him. He's lost to the sickness.'

Water burst through the rotting wood. Within minutes, it was rising fast around them all. 'We have to get to safety,' Whisper shouted.

They swam up to the main deck where Holly and Herbert were waiting, but their faces said it all.

Behind them a wall of water was pouring into the maze, washing it away.

Holly looked frightened. 'Now what do we do?'

Ebony and her crew were on board, soaking wet.

'THIS IS YOUR FAULT, VULCAN!' she said before turning on her crew. 'Get to the secret entrance, quick. Swim down and grab as many barrels of that gold as you can!'

Herbert ran after her. 'It's no good. We checked, but the way is sealed. We are all stuck here.'

Ebony stood alone on the deck, trying to think of a way to get her greedy paws on the precious treasure before it was too late. Meanwhile, Herbert ran back to his friends. They all now stood on board the deck of the *Golden Hind*, with nowhere left to go, waiting for the water to wash them all away.

Just as it looked like it was all over, Whisper grabbed Lupo. 'Wait! I have an idea. We sail her.' No one was sure that this was a good idea. 'Look, I know she's old, but she's got some life left in her yet. If we can just try and steer her out.' Whisper pointed to where the water was pouring in. 'If we can get close enough we might have a slim chance.'

Lupo agreed. 'It's a good idea. Whisper's right. We can sail out but it's going to take all of us working together to sail this boat. There is no crew left, just us. So Vulcan, you and Holly run the sails. Herbert, you can guide us. Ebony, use your crew to get as much off the ship as possible: the lighter she is, the easier she'll float. That means dumping all that gold for starters. Ebony, I mean, *all* of it!'

Vulcan was holding on to a small barrel of gold. Holly walked up to him and pulled it away. 'You have to let go. I'm your friend and I don't want to see you hurt. Please – let's work together and get out of here. If we do get out, I will listen to whatever you have to say. But none of your grand plans will work if you are stuck in this cave.'

She was right, of course. Reluctantly he poured the gold over the side of the ship. Holly patted him on the back. 'You see? That wasn't so bad, was it?'

Vulcan groaned before joining Holly, and together they went to try and heave the massive sails into position.

Ebony had managed to throw great barrels of gold and treasure overboard, telling her crew, 'We'll come back for these. The treasure will be safe in these barrels for now.'

Whisper watched as Ebony's crew began rushing to empty as much of the ship's contents into the water as they could. 'We need to be as light as possible so everything must go! If it's not bolted down, chuck it over!'

Suddenly, the lost pirate felt a rush of excitement. She was ready to go. 'Everyone, I'm going to release the anchor. Once it's gone we should be able to sail away. The ship is lighter now so it might move quickly. Everyone hang on to something.' Everyone ran to grab what they could. 'Are we all ready?'

Lupo ran to her side. 'Whisper, you are one gutsy dog! Let's do it.'

As the anchor broke away, the ship jolted and took off towards the flowing waters. Lupo and Whisper pulled and pushed the wheel of the ship, trying their best to navigate through the gushing water that was pouring in faster and heavier by the second.

Herbert skilfully guided them around a boulder and some rocks, but suddenly the ship crashed into the cave walls, damaging the bow. As the brown mouse clung to the ropes, he saw the cursed gold spilling out of the ship, and then he saw the ship's mascot, the solid gold deer, falling into the water.

'There goes the *Golden Hind*,' he said.

As they came up to the narrow shelf of water, they waited for the level to rise. The noise was so loud that Whisper had to shout. 'THIS IS IT! I'LL DO MY BEST TO STEER HER IN BUT WE WON'T HAVE LONG TO GET HER OUT OR ELSE SHE'LL BE CRUSHED. HANG ON!'

Lupo held on to the helm and Whisper ran to inspect the water level. When the moment had come, she barked as loudly as she could, 'NOW!'

The grand old Elizabethan ship creaked and clattered as it rocked in the fast floodwaters. Whisper knew that they were on the very edge of losing her altogether.

Holly grabbed on to Kitty who was nearby, her eyes closed, praying for a miracle.

The Head of MI5 ran up the mast before stopping near the top to shout. 'It worked, we're out! But we are headed towards a mudslide!'

The watery mud was moving faster and faster. Waves of thick brown mud and water crashed against them again and again.

'SHE'S BREAKING UP, WHISPER. I CAN'T

HOLD HER FOR MUCH LONGER. GET EVERYONE OFF!' Lupo barked as he fought the spinning wheel of the ship.

Whisper gathered everyone together at the bottom of a staircase near the wheel deck. She shouted back to him, 'LUPO, LET GO. I'll TAKE OVER.'

Herbert called out to them all from the mast. 'I can see that there are several pipes coming up. They should take us directly below Kensington Palace. We need to jump into them before we are all splintered to death!'

Kitty rolled her eyes and then pulled on Holly's coat. 'I could've told you he would say something like that. One of these days that mouse is going to kill me and then I'll only have eight lives left!'

Whisper took the wheel from Lupo. 'Go. Take care of your friends. I'll be fine. Go.'

Lupo had never met such a brave dog. Whisper handed him something wrapped in a red bandana. 'Take this, and remember, Lupo: there is nothing more important than your family and friends.'

They were nearing the pipes. Lupo pushed everyone on to the rail at the edge of the ship and one by one they jumped into the pipes. Lupo was the last to go. Whisper waved goodbye and as she did, he jumped. And that was the last anyone ever saw of the legendary *Golden Hind*.

16
Sir Francis Drake's Heart

Lupo's heart felt heavy. Whisper had given her life to save everyone. As a mark of respect, he howled a long deep howl, the kind Whisper would have been proud of, and he hoped that wherever she was, she could hear him.

They had jumped into three different pipes. Vulcan and Ebony had gone with her crew into the first, Holly and Kitty into the second and Herbert and Lupo had only just made it into the last. The pipes were forcing them to ride a rollercoaster of water.

Lupo was far heavier than Herbert and so he managed to catch up with the small mouse. He plucked his friend out of the water. 'Got you!' he said, catching the mouse in his teeth and then pulling

Herbert in close. 'This pipe is taking us all over the place!'

Herbert looked around. 'These pipes haven't been used for a long time.'

The two friends were tossed apart in swirling, rushing water. They carried on flying down the tunnel before being spat out into a man-made river tunnel, running through the underground of a brick building.

Herbert front-crawled to the side of the brickwork and then clambered out on to a wide bank with Lupo behind him. They waited for the others to appear. Lupo could hear Kitty screaming all the way down the pipe that she and Holly had been forced to ride. He underestimated how upset the cat would be when they finally popped out further downstream.

'THAT'S ENOUGH WATER! YUCK! GET ME OUT OF HERE!' the palace cat bellowed.

Graciously Holly pulled Kitty up to the nearest bank. Lupo and Herbert raced to help them both out.

Kitty was very unhappy. 'WHERE IS THE PALACE? I honestly can't take any more.'

Holly, meanwhile, shook herself off.

'Now all we have to do is wait for the rest of them,' said Herbert, looking around.

Ebony, her crew, and Vulcan had not enjoyed being tossed around the narrow pipes leading down to the tunnel under Kensington Palace but at least they were all out now. The black cat meowed, 'FOLLOW THEM!'

Vulcan was in a very bad mood. 'And what exactly are we going to do about the gold? By now it's probably littering the entire sewage system.'

Ebony preened at her cunning plan. 'Chump and Lump, find your way back to the hive. Tell the Crocodile King we've sent his gold downstream. Then send a team to recover the gold from what's left of the cave.'

Vulcan knew it was the only way, so he watched Chump and Lump slithering off. As they left, he felt utterly defeated all over again. He had been so close. This time he had touched the precious gold, rubbed it between his paws and felt its power. He wasn't about to let the Crocodile King take it all. This time he decided to get what he wanted.

'And just where do you think you're going?' Ebony asked.

Vulcan smiled and patted Ebony on her back. 'It's as you said – every dog has its day and mine is today. I'm going to get the gold I need. I'm not coming back until I have all of it.'

Holly turned around to see Vulcan heading after Chump and Lump. 'VULCAN, wait!' she cried.

Lupo tried to stop her. 'Let him go. He'll be back.'

But Holly ran after the royal dorgi until she caught up with him. 'Vulcan, don't go. It's pointless, not to mention dangerous. I can't go back to the palace without you.'

Vulcan turned away from Holly. 'Tell the other corgis, goodbye. Holly, I'm not going back to Buckingham Palace.'

Lupo, Herbert and Kitty stood behind Holly, watching. They were shocked to see the look of determination in the royal dorgi's face.

Holly began to cry. 'Vulcan, no. You can't do this. The Queen will be so upset if you don't come back.'

Vulcan growled, 'Believe me, she won't even notice I've gone. She is only interested in you, Holly. Now let me go.' He pushed her out of his way.

Holly fell to the floor. Vulcan, seeing the sadness

in Holly's eyes, hastily ran away.

Lupo, Herbert and Kitty rushed to Holly's side. 'He's a coward and he will be back,' said Lupo.

Herbert stood and steadied himself. 'Come on,' he said. 'Let's get going. The City of Creatures is that way, then it's a short tunnel ride up to the Red route.'

As the friends walked away, with Ebony and what remained of her crew following, Herbert climbed on to Lupo's ear and said quietly, 'That won't be the last we see of Vulcan.'

Lupo whispered back, 'I have a bad feeling we've just let a bad dog go, and that he'll come back to strike when we least expect it.'

It was a steep uphill climb to the City of Creatures and none of the animals had much strength. Lupo's back leg was very sore. He had managed to hide it for a while, but he could feel it stinging and burning after the last ride down the pipes.

Being mindful of his friends, he pushed away his pain and made his way gingerly behind the others. When they finally arrived back in the city, they were greeted with a big party. The underground animals were all celebrating the end of the storm.

Ebony could see the Katz Bar was doing a brisk trade, thanks to all the visitors. Carefully she slipped into a crowd of cats, her crew following closely behind, leaving the others with the celebrating animals.

'I hate parties, where's the milk?' meowed Kitty.

Lupo couldn't help but laugh. The city had been transformed. 'Where did they all come from?' he asked.

Herbert bowed to welcome several new visitors. 'London Zoo, by the look of it. They must have escaped during the storm and sought refuge down here!'

Strange monkeys swung around the tunnels, and peacocks put on a display of such magnificence that the crowds of mystified animals whooped and cheered. Kitty ducked low when a group of deer darted past them.

Lupo stepped backwards. 'Herbert, we need to get home,' he said quietly.

Holly was in agreement. 'I think we should leave.'

Kitty nodded. 'Home, please. It's a wonderful party but we have been gone a long time and we must get back.'

Herbert would have liked to have stayed very

much. As the others walked away, the little brown mouse ran back to a large monkey who had made himself comfortable in the middle of the market place. He looked like he was in charge. 'We must be getting on but it has been a real high point in my life to have met you.' The monkey looked unimpressed and was squinting to try and see the small creature. Herbert continued, 'I would very much like to return and talk to you about Loch Ness. The monster has been seen.'

The friends found themselves in a new part of Kensington Palace. A sign above the door said 'Tourists and Visitors'. The friends walked through the visitors' kitchen, exhausted and tired from their long adventure. They passed chefs preparing all kinds of pies, cakes and roasted meats. A kind chef put a full bowl of milk in front of Kitty, gave Holly and Lupo a large bone each, and presented Herbert with a piece of cheese. As they all tucked in, relieved to be home, Lupo couldn't help but think of Whisper. 'We need to find Sir Francis. We need to tell him what happened to Whisper.'

'I can take you to him if you like,' said a brown rat sitting in the corner of the room. 'I'm Lenny.'

'I'm Lupo and these are my friends. I haven't seen you here in the visitors' area before.'

Lenny reached out to shake paws with Lupo. 'It's an honour to meet you. We don't get royal animals in this part of Kensington Palace, only the tourists. I've seen Sir Francis sometimes out the back; he seems to like the playground. It's this way.' The others followed the friendly rat. 'What are you guys doing all the way over here anyway? Royal dogs on tour with a cat, I don't quite get it.'

Herbert ran to shake hands with the rat. 'My dear fellow, it really is good to see a friendly face. We've had quite a journey.'

Kitty wasn't nearly as gracious. 'You're a rat. Mice I can just about put up with, but a rat in the palace is more than I can stand.'

Lenny felt around in his jacket pockets. 'I'm not just any rat. Oh good, phewee, here it is,' he said, pulling out a little badge that said:

LENNY – TOUR GUIDE
(PLEASE DO NOT FEED)

'The humans come to visit Kensington Palace in

their thousands. You should see this place during the day, it's crawling with people. No animals, mind you. I never understood why they don't come. Anyway, I know all about the palace because I am a tour guide. Well, I'm not an official tour guide – I just sit on the tour guides' shoulders mostly, you know, as they walk around.' Lupo and his friends looked confused. Lenny shrugged, 'You know, showing the visitors the wonders of Kensington Palace, Queen Victoria's home and stuff.'

'Tour guides? Visitors?' Kitty replied, blowing a disapproving raspberry.

Lenny clapped as he finally understood. 'Hang on. You have never been over to this side of the palace and you're the first live animal visitors EVER! Well, this is a treat. That means that I AM your official guide.'

Kitty was about to pounce on the rat. She was not amused. Seeing her reaction, he stopped laughing.

'OK, someone tell me the cat isn't going to eat me and then I'll take you to the playground to see. Sir Francis.'

Herbert was delighted. 'Oh, this is quite something, Lenny. I have never been on a proper tour before!' Scratching his head, he said, 'Normally, we mice explore everywhere on our own!'

Lenny explained, 'It's a very great pleasure to assist you all. Firstly, let me explain that we have quite a few ghosts here. If we run into Queen Victoria I would suggest you stay very still. She can be quite scary. I have seen her frighten the humans, and she made one girl's hair curl.'

Lenny's tour of the public parts of the palace was incredible. But Lupo was keen to get back to Apartment 1A to see the children.

The little group of animals made their way outside and stopped by the large sculpture of Queen Victoria. She looked splendid in a fine dress, sitting in the middle of a small fountain.

'Lady, cats and dog, and gentle friends, may I present Her Majesty Queen Victoria and our most humble ruler,' Lenny said, with a bow.

The sculpture suddenly moved. It was slowly buckling in the water. The animals stepped back, fearing what was happening. Then a mist began pouring out of it. The mist became thicker and thicker, until standing in front of them stood the spirit of Queen Victoria.

Lupo growled nervously, but the Queen paid him little attention. 'It is my pleasure to have you come and visit my palace.' The animals nodded quietly, still unsure of the old monarch.

'Herbert,' she began, to which Herbert gave a lowly bow. 'You are most welcome at my court any day. You will find the secret passage that connects us all in good time. I will make sure of it. I will send word in a few days to your headquarters, which I have been told are in Hyde Park under the Peter Pan statue?'

Herbert was thrilled. 'Oh yes, Your Majesty is most well informed. May I say that it is most gracious of you to welcome us here. Don't mind my friend Lupo. He is very protective – excuse me, I am gabbling on – I'm just very excited.'

The Queen smiled and bent down towards them all. 'Holly, please pass on my regards to your Queen. From time to time I pop in and look in on her. The poor thing has all that paperwork. Let me tell you it was exactly the same in my reign. I constantly had to deal with those ghastly red despatch boxes!'

Queen Victoria floated towards Lupo. 'All the adventures you've had! So very many for such a young dog,' she said, leaning in so that her white face was looking directly into his brown eyes. 'You are a most unusual royal pet. A warning, Lupo, never ever travel to Hampton Court. There are things that you of all creatures must never see. The fate of many may depend on it.' None of the animals were expecting such a warning. Lupo felt suddenly very uncomfortable in the company of the old Queen. She continued, 'Now, the royal children are in the playground.' Then, as easily as the Queen had appeared, she vanished.

Lupo began running in the direction of the playground barking, 'GEORGE! CHARLOTTE!'

The playground at Kensington Palace is a special place. It's large and filled to bursting with games and hiding places. Kitty, Herbert, Holly and Lupo had never been in it before. They ran in with Lenny, who was trying his best to keep up.

Lupo couldn't see the royal children or his family. He ran through several sandpits and under three rope ladders before spotting a familiar ghost sitting in the corner of the playground looking very sad. 'Sir Francis,' he said.

The ghost of the famous explorer spoke, 'Not now, Lupo.'

'I'm sorry to bother you, but I thought you should know. We found the *Golden Hind*,' said Lupo. Sir Francis stood up. 'And we also found Whisper. She's free now.'

The ghost said nothing and started walking into the middle of the playground. Confused, Lupo followed him. Herbert ran after them both.

Sir Francis stopped and Lupo looked up to see the most splendid pirate ship right in the middle of the playground. And standing on its deck was Whisper. Sir Francis floated up to greet his dog warmly.

As the two ghosts embraced, Herbert spotted two people he knew Lupo would like to see. Running around inside the ship was Prince George, and Princess Charlotte was sitting in the sand pit next to the ship. The Duke and Duchess were laughing together.

'I'm home!' barked Lupo, happily running towards his family.

Holly, Kitty and Lenny stood watching from the slides.

Sir Francis and Whisper glided past Herbert. The kindly ghost said, 'Thank you for finding the lost pirate. You have healed my broken heart. Goodbye.' Then he disappeared with Whisper trotting along by his side.

Droplets of water started to fall from the sky. The rain grew heavy and that was when the real show began. The rain danced across the sky, forming patterns of such wonder they looked like the explosions from a great fireworks display.

Holly was shocked. 'Have you ever? It must be some kind of magic. It's so beautiful.'

The friends all huddled under a large tree to watch Prince George playing on the playground's large pirate ship in his little red wellies. Lupo was running after him, barking. The royal family all cheered with delight beneath their umbrellas.

Kitty sneezed loudly. 'I hate water, I'm going inside. And, for the record, I have had quite enough of boats and adventures to last me what is left of my nine lives!'

* * *

Lupo was happy to be back in the nursery. Holly had gone to Buckingham Palace to try and explain to the others what had happened to Vulcan. Herbert had arranged for them all to meet in the Red route the following day.

The Duke was reading a bedtime story to the children. Lupo snuggled into his royal blanket under Princess Charlotte's cot, and when he fell asleep that night, his dreams were filled with all the adventures he had shared with his friends.

The following morning, Tommy the mouse was mending the tapestry Ebony had damaged. Herbert stood watching Tommy weave miracles and repair the priceless artwork. Lupo, Holly and Kitty stood behind him, admiring the picture in front of them.

Herbert bowed. 'This, everyone, is all that remains of the *Golden Hind*.'

Lupo stared at the tapestry, completely transfixed. 'I wonder where . . .' he began, before stopping and pointing at the tapestry. 'Is that who I think it is?' All the friends stood together and watched as the *Golden Hind* and all its ghostly crew joined the rest of the boats in the picture. On the main deck was Sir Francis Drake and standing next to him was a young boy and one shaggy grey dog. 'It is! Everyone look, it's Whisper!'

Herbert thanked Tommy. 'After the tapestry was damaged, I asked Tommy to come and repair it and make some changes. I hope that wherever she sails, the crew and the *Golden Hind* have a wonderful adventure.'

Herbert passed something to Lupo. 'I managed to save this in the pipe. I thought you might want it.' It was Whisper's red bandana. They all ran ahead to see what was inside it. Carefully Lupo untied the little package of cloth to find a beautifully carved wooden dog inside.

Lupo smiled. 'Come on, let's get home. Princess Charlotte wants to teach us all how to play snakes and ladders. Herbert, do you want to join us?'

'Snakes and Ladders? No thanks! I've only just got that Python out of my mind!'

Kitty was busy cleaning herself. Licking one paw and wiping it behind her left ear, she said, 'I've got a bone to pick with you, Herbie. Don't think I didn't hear you inviting Lenny to Buckingham Palace for a visit. He'd better not think that the invitation is extended to our apartment at Kensington Palace. If I

see that crazy rat thinking he can just hop over to my
side of the palace I'll . . .'

17
Moving Day

Claw had been secretly following Chump and Lump by keeping hidden in the shadows. He was surprised to see how dedicated they were and how easily they had found the barrels of cursed gold. What he wasn't expecting was to see Vulcan digging furiously in the thick clay. The royal dog had changed; he wasn't the spoilt dog he had come to know. When their backs were turned, Vulcan was taking piles of gold from Chump and Lump. If the Crocodile King under the Thames knew that Vulcan was stealing from him, there would certainly be trouble. In Claw's opinion, Vulcan had become very foolish indeed and he was treading a fine line. One wrong move and that nasty looking Chump would have his skinny legs for dinner.

Edgar the raven had decided to come and see just how much gold Vulcan was hiding from the others. He had been hoping for a long time to get there. He had no choice now his wings were clipped, but he had managed to get all the way down to Vulcan's lair and he was feeling pretty proud of himself.

'Claw, is your family ready?' he asked the snivelling buck rat. 'If I can hop all the way down here, they should have no problems and be twice as fast!'

'Yes, master,' answered Claw. 'He won't be going anywhere without us knowing about it. But can I ask you a question?' he asked, putting up his paw.

'What is it?' replied Edgar.

'Why is it, again, that we can't destroy him and take the gold all for ourselves?'

'Because he has a plan and we don't know it yet. I want to know what he is intending to do with all that gold. Besides, we are not in the business of destroying royal dogs. That is the job of the Crocodile King,' said Edgar confidently.

Vulcan was ready to move his gold at last and his new crew was right on time.

The tunnel filled with a sudden cold blackness. The waters at his feet began to move and churn.

Thousands of the blackest rats appeared with rafts, ready to carry the gold to its new home. 'Load it up, boys. It's time to get going,' Vulcan ordered.

Edgar watched with Claw from a distance. 'Vulcan has no idea we are behind this?' Claw asked.

'No, he doesn't know he is walking into a trap,' said Edgar, gleefully. 'It's almost sad. The Queen has lost her dorgi until I'm ready to return him. Stay on it, Claw. I want regular reports of his progress. And how is everything at Balmoral?'

It was far worse than Edgar could have imagined, Claw was worried about giving him the bad news. 'Sir, he has a monster there and I think he means to use it.'

'A monster you say? Well, Claw, it looks like Lupo isn't going to be as quiet in the countryside as we had originally thought. I just hope he's getting some rest because his next adventure could very well be his last now that Vulcan has the upper hand.'

Percy the Pigeon was sitting outside the nursery window. Dawn's first sun rays were bursting over the palace gardens. He looked up to where the weathervane on the roof of the palace was swinging all the way to the left, sending a golden ray in his direction.

'Morning, Percy.' Lupo poked his head out of the window, giving the pigeon quite a scare. 'What's the latest?'

Percy was so shocked to see the royal dog that he flapped his wings wildly, sending feathers falling everywhere. 'Lupo! I'll be glad when you're too far away to scare me like that again!' A single feather landed on the end of Lupo's nose. 'It's moving day, Lupo. That's what! The trucks have been coming all morning. You'd better be ready because you're leaving for the Norfolk countryside this morning,' pecked the busy bird. 'And that means I get my palace back. Nice and quiet. No more of your crazy antics!'

Lupo could see the trucks parked up outside the front of the palace. His heart felt heavy. He was going to miss Kensington Palace. Bernie the Head Mousekeeper was scooting around the nursery, picking up toys that had been lost, and crossing things off her long list. Lupo stuck his nose under the blue sofa, just in time to hear her shouting out instructions to a large team of palace mice, 'Remember everyone, the family leave this afternoon and I want this place closed up the minute they go, so that means nothing must be left behind!'

Kitty was nowhere in sight. He'd hoped to see her to say goodbye before they left. She had been very quiet ever since they had come back from their adventure to find the *Golden Hind*. He hoped he might find her in the kitchen.

When he walked in, he saw that the Duke was sipping a cup of coffee at the breakfast table. 'Everyone packed?' asked the Duke. Prince George clapped loudly. 'That's right, we are all off for a new adventure. There's no need to look so sad, Lupo. Just think of all the walks on the beach we can have!' the Duke said, patting Lupo on the head.

Lupo left them sitting in the kitchen, finishing their breakfast. Charlotte was happily eating a yoghurt with Nanny, and George was running around, unable to contain his excitement.

Lupo walked to the hallway. The Duchess was talking to a man near the front door. In his arms was the magnificent model of the *Golden Hind*. 'You will take good care of it, won't you?' she asked.

'Oh yes, it's going to be very well cared for.'

'Goodbye and best of luck with the move, Your Royal Highness. London will miss you all,' said the man as he left.

The Duchess waved the man off and shut the door behind him. Lupo saw Kitty sitting at the top of the main staircase, looking downcast.

'Lupo! Boy, am I glad to see you. Come here, I want to have a word,' the Duchess said, sitting down on the bottom stair. 'The Duke and I have been talking. We know how much you love her, so we thought we might take Kitty with us to Norfolk. Do you think she might like to come? She can keep you company!'

Lupo wagged his tail, then looked up and noticed that Kitty was gone.

'Come on then. Nanny is taking George for one last walk around the park. Why don't you go with them whilst I finish the packing? You can go and find Kitty and tell her the good news later.'

Lupo sat down on the marble floor next to the elegant Duchess. She ran her slim hand over his face, 'Come on, Lupo, cheer up. I know saying goodbye to this place is hard but it's not forever. We'll be back.'

Epilogue

The headstones in the garden on the edge of the park were small. They were also very closely packed together. Nanny reached out and caught Prince George's hand as he tried to follow Lupo.

'Don't get too close, George, this is where people in the olden times buried their beloved pets. It's one of London's best kept secrets!' Nanny said, leaning into the buggy and wiping Princess Charlotte's nose at the same time.

Lupo had heard of Hyde Park's pet cemetery but had never seen it until today. He had walked past it many times without realising that it was even there.

Something was pulling him forwards. He lowered his head respectfully and walked amongst the small headstones, reading out the names of the dogs and cats that had been so lovingly remembered.

MY DARLING IGGY FOREVER 1808

RUFFLES OUR FRIEND 1887

SWEET PHOEBE ALWAYS LOYAL 1894

THE WORLD'S BEST DOG *HERA* WITH
LOVE AND THANKS 1882

ALWAYS REMEMBERED COCO 1901

Then he noticed one right at the very back. He went over to it and wiped away the moss that was covering what remained of the inscription. There was one word on it and it said . . .

WHISPER

Lupo sat down in front of it and he then reached out and touched it with his paw. 'Goodbye, dear friend and thank you. Rest in peace.'

Have you read . . . ?

Lupo and the Secret of Windsor Castle

Lupo is out for a walk with Nanny and Prince George in
Kensington Gardens when he is lured into a wicked trap.
Cyrus the swan has been attacked, and some precious
royal treasure stolen. Lupo is innocent but can he prove
it? Meanwhile, his rival, Vulcan the corgi is plotting to
take over the realm. Animals take sides in a classic battle
of good versus evil, involving journeys through
underground tunnels and down the hallowed corridors
of historic palaces.

Don't miss . . .

Lupo and the Curse
at Buckingham Palace

It's the Queen's birthday, and the palace is ready to
celebrate. But the discovery of an ancient curse threatens
to spoil the plans – for ever. Can Lupo and his friends
get to the bottom of a mysterious curse which was
brought to Buckingham Palace from ancient Egypt?
That is – before Vulcan gets his paws on it! And this
time, brave Lupo faces another opponent in the form of
a sleek and formidable queen cat called Ebony who has
designs on becoming the next queen of England.

Another brilliant adventure . . .

Lupo and the Thief
at the Tower of London

The royal family are disturbed by the shocking news that
there has been a break-in at the Tower of London –
everything has been stolen, including the crown jewels.
The adults say it's a human matter, but Lupo has an
especially bad feeling about this particular crime. He and
Kitty take matters into their own hands. Meanwhile,
something is stirring in the Thames – a creature who has
been hiding in the sewers for hundreds of years.

A creature with revenge on its mind . . .